THE KRISHNA CHRONICLES

The Story of Krishna & the Pandav Princes

Inspired by

The Mahabharat and Harivansh

An ancient text from India

By

Sudhir Joglekar

The Krishna Chronicles

World Edition:
8th December 2020

Indian Edition
30th November 2024

Published by
R.C. Joglekar for Omega Publications
2 & 3 Emerald Corner, Maratha Colony,
Tilakwadi, Belagavi, Karnataka, India 590 006

Corespondence:
#40, Yashwant Vihar, Nanawadi, Belagavi 590 009
Email: omegapress@gmail.com
Cell : +91 988 620 3256

Cover Credits
Sudhir Joglekar, Fiona, U.K.

Price : Rs. 250/-

ISBN 978-81-967131-1-9

Dedicated to the fond remembrance of my parents who instilled in me a love for books and languages.

Contents

Author's Preface 5
Acknowledgments 7
Krishna Family Tree 8
Kuru Dynasty Family Tree 9
Map of India during Mahabharat period 10
1. Proposal from Paradise 11
2. Miracle in Mathura 17
3. Growing up in Gokul 25
4. Valor in Vraj 32
5. Triumph in Mathura 38
6. Destination Dwarika 46
7. The Jewel Thief 53
8. Panchali and the Pandavs 62
9. From Rags to Riches 70
10. A Sister's Solace 78
11. Of Wives and Vines 90
12. Justice for Jarasandh 100
13. Shenanigans of Shishupal 111
14. The War at Dwarika 120
15. The Empty Bowl 128
16. The Mediator 135
17. A Mother's Maledictions 151
18. Dwarika Doomed 159
19. About the Author 178

Preface

The thought for writing this book germinated when I realized, while chatting with several friends from the West on social media, that the average reader from the Occident is not aware of the existence of The Mahabharat and The Ramayan, the great epics from India, that have enthralled readers for more than three thousand years and continue to do so even today.

The first edition, World edition, had some features particularly meant for readers from abroad who are not conversant with traditional Indian names. Several friends desired that the book be published in a form suitable for Indian teens who are increasingly attending English-medium schools and do not have authentic knowledge of our epics. Hence this edition with names as they appear in the original epic.

The Mahabharat is one of the oldest Sanskrit epics of ancient India. It is also the longest known epic poem. It consists of about a hundred thousand verses. That makes it roughly four times the length of The Ramayan. The importance of The Mahabharat to world civilization has been compared to the works of Shakespeare, or those of Homer.

The epic is traditionally ascribed to Sage Vyas, who is also a major character in the epic. Over the millennia a host of authors have added numerous stories and angles to the main story and the result has been quite absorbing. The original is believed to be a work of history titled The Jaya. However, the historicity of the Kurukshetra War is unclear. There is much difference of opinion about the date of the war, as well as that of the penning of the epic. A dynastic conflict of the period could have been the inspiration for The Jaya.

On its surface, the core story of the work is that of a dynastic struggle for the throne of Hastinapur. The two collateral branches of the Kuru clan that participate in the struggle are the Kauravs and the Pandavs. The struggle culminates in the great war of Kurukshetra. The battle produces complex conflicts of kinship and friendship, instances of family loyalty and duty taking precedence over what is right, as well as the converse. It raises complex questions of what is good and what evil, and whether the end justifies the means. One of the Pandav brothers asks, just before the beginning of the battle, if the suffering caused by war can ever be justified. A long discussion ensues which results in the text considered holy by the Hindus, The Gita.

The Mahabharat theorizes about a "just war", establishing criteria like proportionality, just means, just cause, and fair treatment of captives and the wounded. However, both sides transgress these limits in the heat of battles, giving rise to the question of unethical means for a just end. Thus, the story of the warring cousins is transformed into the eternal struggle between the Good and Evil on one level, and the struggle between Man's Destiny and Deeds on another level.

Indeed, there are several books based on the epic, as well as the translation of the whole text available in English. However, the main text is too lengthy and meandering with its story within story structure. Also, some of the books which recount the entire story in modern English are voluminous and forbidding, some are written from the perspective of particular characters, some from a spiritual angle. These, I thought, would not serve as an introductory book for the uninitiated. So I decided to render only the central story related to the main heroes in an adventure form first. The stories of other major characters, which are also fascinating, I have brought out in the current sequel.

The central book "Adventures of the Pandav Princes" was published first. Now this sequel "Krishna Chronicles" is being released. Krishna's story is not really a sequel to the story of Pandavs but is a parallel one. However, with a view to restrict the number of pages I did not include Krishna's story in the Pandav book. It is being published as a separate book now. Since a large portion of the two books overlaps some repetition became unavoidable. Another advantage is that this enables readers to read both books as stand alones too.

I intend to soon bring out the prequel to both these books, 'The Kings of Yore,' containing the stories of the ancestors of the Pandavs.

If this retelling generates interest in The Mahabharat in the minds of the reader, I shall consider my efforts fulfilled.

30th November 2024 — ***– Sudhir Joglekar***

Yudhishthir Ascention Day

Acknowledgments

My heartfelt thanks are due to my senior friend Vasant Inamdar, my young friend Rutuja Kamat, Beatrice Mollo from Italy, and Fiona from UK, for the support and valuable suggestions offered throughout the writing of the book. Fiona also helped with the graphics for the book.

I acknowledge with gratitude the meticulous reading and helpful inputs from beta readers Linda White of U.K., Emily Horn, and late Mary Endersbe from the USA whose untimely passing away was very saddening.

I remember with gratitude the Late Prof. Dr. V.P. Ginde for going through the book and offering valuable suggestions regarding the contents.

A special mention must be made of Late Shri. Ashok Yalgi of Lokmanya Library, who readily procured every book I requested for reference.

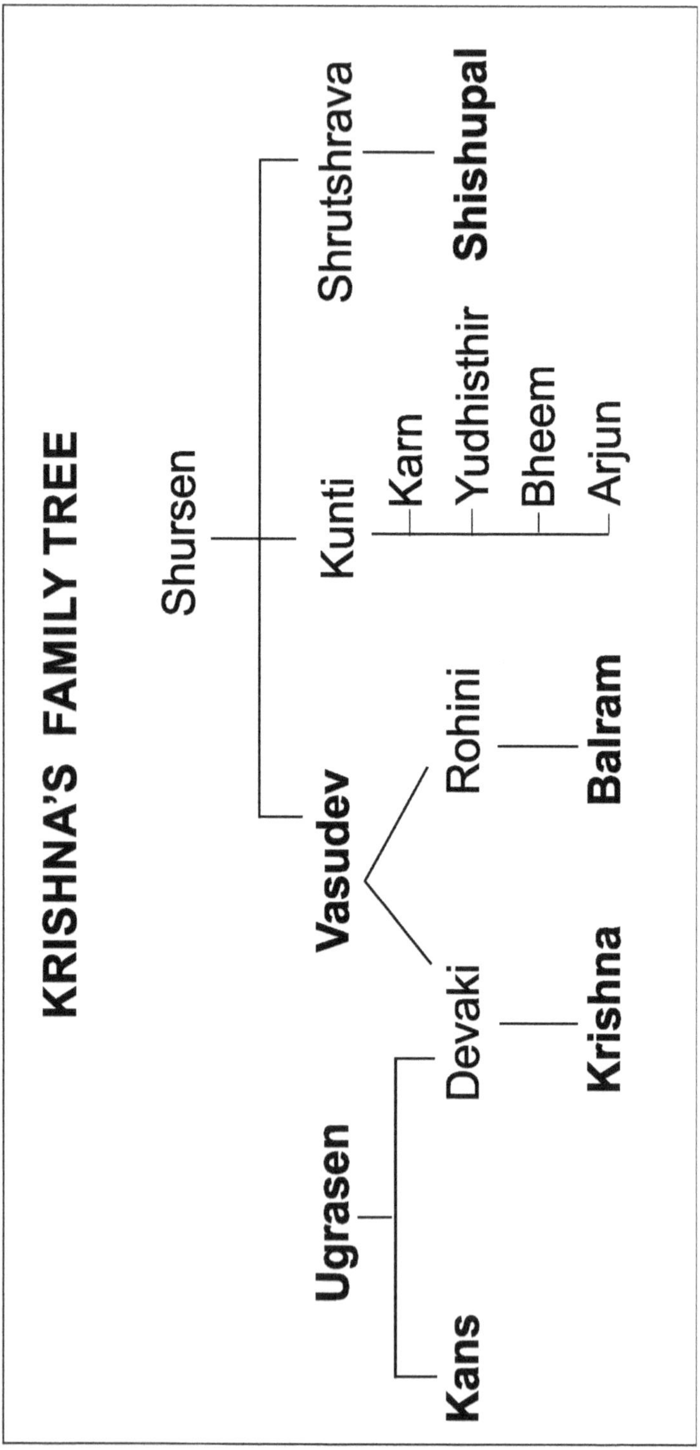
KRISHNA'S FAMILY TREE
Shursen
Vasudev
Kunti
Shrutshrava
Rohini
Balram
Devaki
Krishna
Karn
Yudhisthir
Bheem
Arjun
Shishupal
Ugrasen
Kans

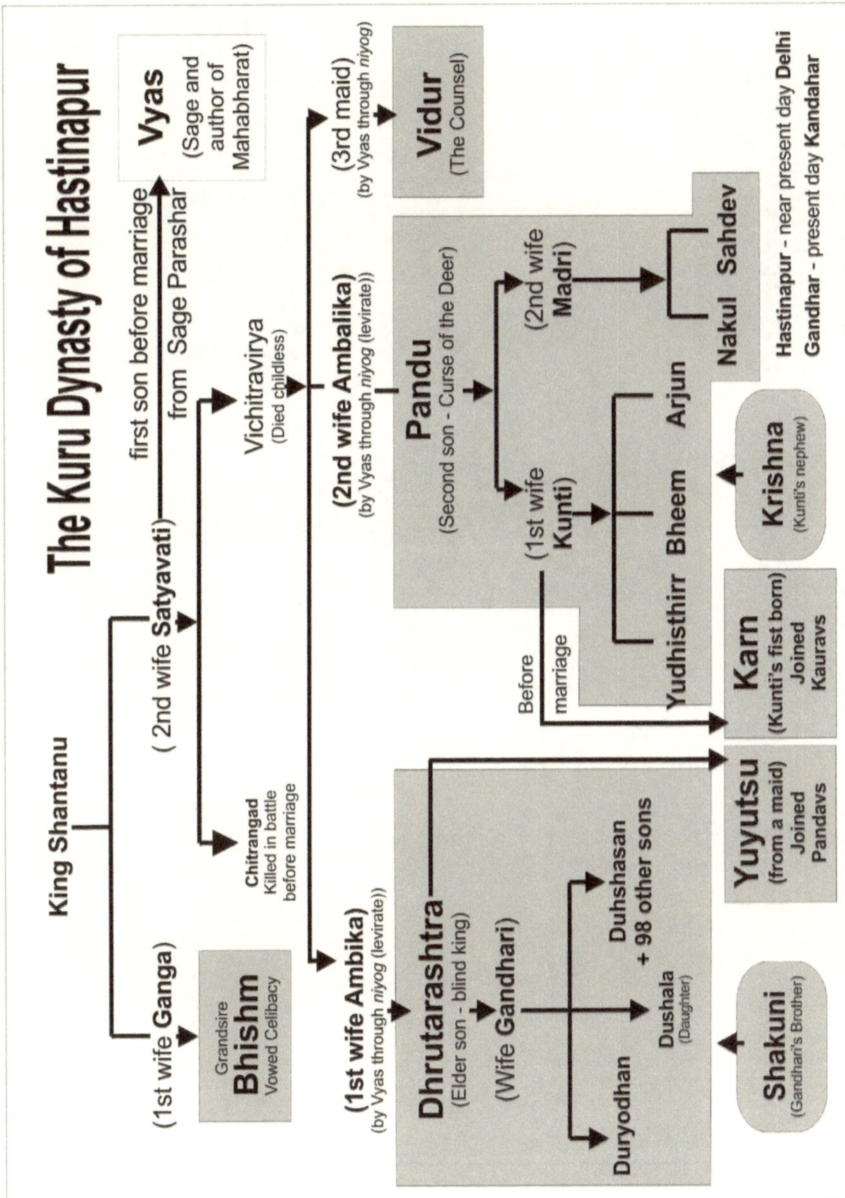
The Kuru Dynasty of Hastinapur
King Shantanu
(1st wife Ganga)
Grandsire
Bhishm
Vowed Celibacy
(2nd wife Satyavati)
first son before marriage
from Sage Parashar
Vyas
(Sage and author of Mahabharat)
Chitrangad
Killed in battle before marriage
Vichitravirya
(Died childless)
(1st wife Ambika)
(by Vyas through niyog (levirate))
(2nd wife Ambalika)
(by Vyas through niyog (levirate))
(3rd maid)
(by Vyas through niyog)
Dhrutarashtra
(Elder son - blind king)
(Wife Gandhari)
Duryodhan
Dushala
(Daughter)
Duhshasan
+ 98 other sons
Pandu
(Second son - Curse of the Deer)
(1st wife Kunti)
(2nd wife Madri)
Yudhisthirr
Bheem
Arjun
Nakul
Sahdev
Vidur
(The Counsel)
Before marriage
Karn
(Kunti's fist born)
Joined Kauravs
Yuyutsu
(from a maid)
Joined Pandavs
Shakuni
(Gandhari's Brother)
Krishna
(Kunti's nephew)
Hastinapur - near present day Delhi
Gandhar - present day Kandahar

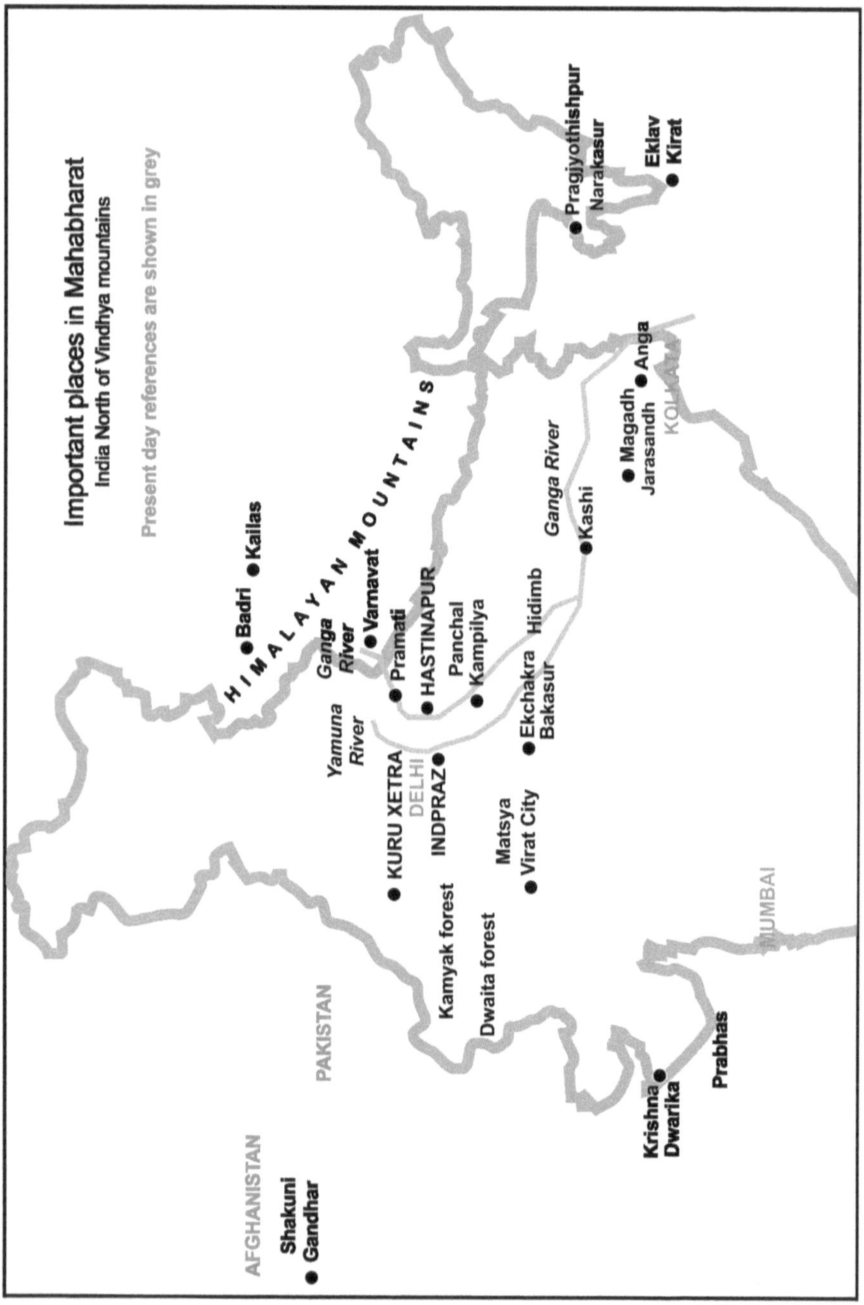
Important places in Mahabharat
India North of Vindhya mountains
Present day references are shown in grey
HIMALAYAN MOUNTAINS
Badri
Kailas
Vamavat
Ganga River
Pramati
HASTINAPUR
Panchal
Kampilya
Hidimb
Ganga River
Kashi
Magadh
Jarasandh
Anga
KOLKATA
Pragjyothishpur
Narakasur
Eklav
Kirat
Yamuna River
KURU XETRA
DELHI
INDPRAZ
Ekchakra
Bakasur
Matsya
Virat City
Kamyak forest
Dwaita forest
PAKISTAN
MUMBAI
Prabhas
Krishna
Dwarika
AFGHANISTAN
Shakuni
Gandhar

1. Proposal from Paradise

It began as a normal day in the court of King Ugrasen of the Yadavs in the capital city. Mathura, the city of charming gardens, on the banks of river Yamuna, basked in the autumn sun. The morning had begun well enough with reports of his son Kans' victory. He had sent Kans to put down the bandits in the northern part of the kingdom and messengers had arrived informing him that Prince Kans was returning to the capital after a successful mission.

However, Ugrasen's elation was short-lived. As soon as he took his high seat in the richly decorated court his old minister spoke to him.

"A delegation of the prominent citizens has arrived, my lord," he began in a grave manner, "they wish to speak about some urgent matter."

At a nod from the king, the sentries ushered the delegates. Citizens were always received courteously at the Yadav king's court.

"My lord," their leader, a rich merchant, began in a solemn voice, "the citizens of Mathura are very happy under your rule. You are impartial, fair, and swift in imparting justice; kind and considerate in collection of taxes, and always pay heed to the advice and opinions of your citizens."

"Speak your mind freely, sir," the king assured him cutting his tedious preamble short.

"It is about the prince, my lord," another delegate, a learned teacher, ventured.

"I hear he is victorious in his mission," the king said with some pride, "I am thinking of appointing him crown prince when he returns."

"Indeed, he has achieved victory," a third delegate, a high priest, spoke, "but I must say, he has departed from your noble tradition."

"In what way?" the king wasn't too happy to hear this.

"He has unleashed terror among the citizens," he blurted out, "his cruel ways are unprecedented. He has tortured the innocent along with the culprits. He has not spared even women and children. He has no faith in taking prisoners. He has executed hundreds. Mass executions are common under him."

King Ugrasen was taken aback by this accusation. He looked at the minister.

"There is truth in what they say, my lord. News from reliable sources has preceded the Prince of his deeds in the north."

"This is outrageous! I was on the verge of appointing him crown prince today! I am saved. The council of elders shall not ratify him now." The distraught King stroked his grey beard, as he thought aloud.

The Yadav kingdom practised a particular type of democracy. It comprised several clans, and the chiefs of these clans appointed the king. If the king named a successor, he had to be ratified by the chiefs.

"My lord," another minister spoke up, "the matter does not end here. Prince Kans has the support of King Jarasandh of Magadh. His insolence rests on the might of Magadh."

Prince Kans had recently married the twin daughters of Jarasandh. Jarasandh had not hidden his ambitions of becoming the emperor of Aryavart. He had chosen his ally well in Kans.

The king sat brooding. The minister and nobles looked at each other. An uneasy silence followed. The hurried footsteps of the sentry at the entrance rang on the polished floor shattering the silence. He came close to the minister, bowed and whispered. The king gave the minister an enquiring look.

"My lord, prince Kans along with his elite troops is at the city gates. He is expected here soon."

There was murmur among the nobles in the court. The king, in an attempt to cover his discomfort, tried to continue the day's work. He asked the minister to present the next matter. But no one could concentrate on that agenda. Everyone waited in anticipation.

There was some commotion at the entrance to the court hall. Then the prince entered with long strides. His personal guards followed. Prince Kans stood in the middle of the open space in front of the king, but the king did not care to look at him.

"The king is not pleased with my victory?" Kans asked with a scowl on his swarthy face.

King Ugrasen raised his eyes slowly and stared at his son. "The Yadav kingdom has a culture and tradition of respecting its innocent citizens, honouring its ladies and sparing its children..."

"I know, sire, but..." Kans exhibited his impatience.

"In view of your rash actions," the king continued as if he had not been interrupted, "I have decided not to appoint you crown prince until you mend your ways..."

"Ha! I don't care for that post!" Kans, taking deliberate steps towards the throne, interrupted again. His face turned ugly and his eyes were bloodshot. "I deserve to be the king! Step down and hand me the crown, father! You have become senile and should retire now!"

Kans turned around and signalled to his men who instantly drew their weapons and took positions. The king, as well as the noblemen present, was stunned at his insolence. As the speechless king continued to stare at him in disbelief, Kans waved his hand impatiently, "Are you going to hand me the crown or should I take it?" He moved threateningly closer. The king got up from his seat and with shaky hands he removed his crown and handed it over to his son. He stood awkwardly not knowing what to do. Kans threw his own headgear on the floor and donned the crown. He sat on the throne clutching the armrests and looked at his father for a few moments, thinking.

"Escort his lordship to the retreat home and guard him well," Kans ordered the captain of the guards, adding as an afterthought, "See that my father gets all the amenities. He needs rest in his old age."

It all happened so fast, the noblemen had no time to think. That Kans had the backing of the mighty Jarasandh of Magadh was at the back of their minds. They remained silent spectators as the drama unfolded.

That evening Kans sat in his quarters sipping wine. His two wives sat with him. A chanteuse made melody in the palace garden below his window. But his mind was occupied with the happenings of the day. The Yadav noblemen had not resisted his takeover of the throne, yet they were not supportive either. He needed some of them on his side. He abruptly rang for the servant.

"Summon Lord Vasudev," he ordered. He turned to his queens, "We will be discussing court matters, my dears." They understood his meaning and left for their chambers.

Kans got up and paced the floor. Vasudev was his friend since childhood. He belonged to the Vrishni tribe of the Yadavs while Kans was from the Bhoj. He had a good standing among the noblemen. But he was also close to Kans' father. If Kans could win over Vasudev, his own standing would improve considerably among the Vrishnis.

"Lord Vasudev has arrived," the servant informed.

The two friends embraced as Vasudev entered. Kans offered him a seat and a cool drink.

"You have been my close friend and confidante since long, Vasu." Kans came straight to the point. "And now I want our relation to be even closer." Vasudev waited as Kans smiled. "I offer Devaki, my sister in marriage to you."

Vasudev was taken aback by this unexpected development.

"But, my dear friend," he said, "I am already married to Rohini."

"I know, I know," Kans smiled broadly, "but is your heart so tiny that two women cannot dwell in it? My father too will approve of you as his son-in-law."

Vasudev thought quickly. He realized the political motive behind the offer. He was in two minds. In a way this could distance him from Ugrasen, but at the same time it could strengthen his bonds with the royal family and help him protect the deposed king from further harm.

Vasudev nodded his assent to Kans' proposal half-heartedly. Kans embraced him with great joy. He ordered his servant to serve sweets. He immediately sent for the priest to find an auspicious day for the nuptials.

A day was fixed and invitations, inscribed in golden letters, sent to all the important lords of the various tribes of the Yadavs. The city of Mathura was decorated. On the appointed day Kans married away his sister Devaki to Vasudev in a grand ceremony.

***

The Lord of Elysium shivered as he plunged deep into Netherworld. The dark and cold waters there were in stark contrast to the warm and pleasant ambience of his abode in upper Elysium. Today he had a mission to accomplish in this subterranean world. Ignoring the malevolent glances of profanity-muttering denizens of Netherworld he straggled through the swales dotted with twisted trunks of trees with lethal foliage.

In a cave he saw demonic souls of six brothers lying in murky water, waiting for their turn to take birth on earth. A thoughtful expression crossed his countenance. He passed the cave and suddenly he spotted what he was looking for.

She was resting on a flat stone at the mouth of a gully. The deity of sleep seemed to be drowsing. Her unkempt hair hung loose, half-covering her bare torso. She wore a skirt of animal skin which reached her knees. She must have spotted his radiant celestial raiment through her long droopy eyelids, for she quietly retreated into the gulley. The Lord followed her with quick steps.

"What do you want, O Great Lord?" she turned to face him.

"I came with the express purpose of seeing you, Deity of Sleep."

"Why?"

"I have a proposal."

"What proposal?" The demigoddess eyed him suspiciously.

"The proposal will set you free from the murky depths of the Netherworld. You shall live the glorious life of a great goddess in the mountainous regions on the earth."

"What's the catch?" She knew all about the schemes of gods.

"There is no catch, I assure you," he sounded sincere enough. "All you have to do is take birth in the line of the chief of the cowherds in the kingdom of Mathura."

"And...?"

"It will be a short life of just one day, and then you will be set free and worshipped as a goddess of the mountains."

"Do I have a choice, O Lord?"

"It's not a bad proposal; I will see you soon as a baby

girl in the household of the cowherd." The Lord's smile was disarming. "And now take charge of those six demonic souls lying in the cave. They too will have a short role to play."

"You know what is best for the three worlds, O Great Lord." The demigoddess bowed in acceptance.

His mission accomplished the Great Lord left for his abode in the milky ocean of heaven. As he reclined on his bed in the coils of the celestial serpent, he whispered, "We are going to visit earth soon."

"As you please, my lord," the gargantuan multi-headed snake replied.

"We will take birth as brothers in a village in the kingdom of Mathura."

2. Miracle in Mathura

"Narayan, Narayan." The celestial sage Narad sat in the court of the Celestial Lord chanting the Lord's name in tune to the *Veena* hung around his neck. His head was shaven clean with only a tuft of hair on the crest. His forehead was adorned with stripes of sandal paste. He was a unique wandering minstrel, who roamed earth, netherworld and heaven and carried news from one world to the other. Whenever he saw potential for a dilemma, he first precipitated it and then resolved it. That is why people received this Veena-strumming sage with mixed emotions of apprehension and admiration. Narad had landed early in the morning at heaven. He had been received by the gods with due respect. He sat with the gods, who asked him about news from the earth.

"The earth is reeling under the atrocities committed by King Jarasandh and his son in law King Kans," he intoned in his nasal voice. "Jarasandh has the ambition to be emperor of Aryavart. He is subjugating one King after another and imprisoning those who don't acquiesce. He has jailed scores of princes and plans to perform human sacrifice when the number reaches a hundred. Kans has unleashed a reign of terror on his own subjects. The chiefs of Yadav tribe have meekly accepted him although in their heart of hearts they despise his rule."

"Yes, Lord," the gods addressed the Great Lord Vishnu supporting what Narad had said, "we too have heard of the duo's misdeeds."

"A number of demons are taking birth in the line of various kings," Indra, the ruler of lower Elysium said, "I have received news from my sources."

"These demons shall join the forces of evil on earth. You must find a solution soon," Brahma, the grandfather of the gods appealed to Lord Vishnu.

"I am aware of these developments and have a plan," the Great Lord smiled at the gods and sages assembled. "In the eighth year from now, on the eighth day of the dark fortnight, I shall take birth in the line of Vasudev and Devaki in Mathura and shall cause the destruction of both Kans and Jarasandh. In a great war at the end of the epoch, I shall also cause the demise of all the demons who are now taking birth on earth."

Sage Narad heard this from the Lord himself and was delighted that he could now sow dissent in Kans' land. He bowed to the Great Lord and left the heaven in a hurry. The Lord looked at the departing sage and smiled to himself knowing he would be up to fresh mischief.

Passing swiftly by aerial route through the seven echelons of heaven, Narad alighted in a grove outside Mathura and sat under a banyan tree. He sent word to Kans and waited strumming his Veena.

As soon as Kans got the sage's message he hurried to meet the revered sage. He paid obeisance to Narad and enquired of his well-being.

"I am well, thank you, Kans," Narad replied. "It is you whose well-being I am worried about."

"Oh, why do you say so, sire?" Kans was taken aback by Narad's words. "Am I in danger?"

"Listen carefully. I have been to a meeting of the gods in the celestial city. Your nemesis shall take birth in the line of your friend Vasu, in the womb of your own sister Devaki! The gods have planned this..."

Kans was stunned. He realized he had inadvertently dug his own grave by marrying off Devaki to Vasu.

"Take precautions!" Narad said as he took his leave strumming the Veena. He was very pleased with himself for planting the tormenting thought in Kans' mind.

Kans returned to his palace deep in speculation. After considerable brain-storming he evolved a plan. He sent for the captain of his trusted guards and the head of eunuchs in his palace.

"I want Vasudev and Devaki watched round the clock. Detail sentries around their mansion. Have them followed everywhere," he instructed the captain.

Then he turned to the eunuch, "Appoint a couple of trusted female servants and eunuchs in Devaki's quarters. I want to know when Devaki misses her period, and the progress of her pregnancy."

News of Narad's arrival, prophecy of Kans' fate and his plan to evade his destiny spread in no time in whispers in the capital from sentries and eunuchs. Vasudev and Devaki too became aware of the danger. They noticed the sentries around their home. They realized they were prisoners in their own home. However, there was little they could do about it.

As days, weeks and months passed, Kans waited in anxiety. One fine morning the Great Lord quietly sent a word to the Deity of Sleep to send one of the six demonic souls in her possession to Devaki's womb. Then one day, the head of the eunuchs arrived with the news that Devaki was definitely pregnant.

As the eighth month passed, Kans received reports about Devaki's condition every day. He had the chariot stand by. On the fateful day as Devaki went in labour, news was conveyed to Kans. When he arrived at Vasudev's mansion, Devaki had already given birth to the baby. He entered the labour room, with a trembling Vasu following him. Devaki clutched the baby to her bosom in haste. But Kans was too fast and strong for her. Before Vasudev could act, he snatched away the baby and hurled it against the wall with such force that only a splash of blood and tissue remained.

"You fiend!" Devaki shrieked, "What sort of a brother are you?"

Kans laughed aloud. "The scriptures say, a person has the right to kill to protect himself. I have acted in self defence! Your child is supposed to be my scourge... how can I let it live?"

He stormed out of Vasudev's residence, relieved that his plan was working. He reinforced the sentries and servants on duty in the Vasudev household, which had now become a virtual prison. To be sure, after a couple of months had passed, news arrived of Devaki's pregnancy again. Once again Kans went to their home and smashed the baby to a pulp.

Six times the drama unfolded in Vasudev's mansion. Each time helpless Devaki and Vasudev grieved and Kans laughed. All six of the demonic souls were thus destroyed by Kans without him being aware of who they were. It was then that the Great Lord ordered the celestial serpent to enter Devaki's womb, and she became pregnant the seventh time.

This time around Devaki asked Vasu, "How long will these horrendous episodes continue? I am sick to the core of the wails of our babies. I can take this no more. If our child does not survive, how will it end the unjust reign of Kans?"

"Yes, we will have to come up with a plan," Vasudev said, his forehead furrowed in thought. He consulted a trusted seer who gave him a secret potion. When Devaki was in her eighth month, one night Vasudev made his two wives, the senior Rohini and Devaki, sit together.

"Drink this potion, both of you," he offered them. They both drank it from crystal vessels.

As the two sat together waiting, a light ray emerged from Devaki and entered Rohini.

"I feel my belly light again!" Devaki exclaimed.

"And I feel mine heavy!" Rohini smiled.

The embryo had been transferred from Devaki's womb to Rohini's.

"Rohini, go to my friend Nand, the chief of cowherds in Gokul village," Vasudev told her. "He will be our haven in these difficult times."

Since the sentries had not been asked to watch Rohini, she left the house quietly next morning. She crossed the river Yamuna in a boat and went to the village of Gokul on the other bank. She met Nand who was the chief there. He offered her a place to live. She stayed in a small house next to Chief Nand's and waited.

The maids in Devaki's quarters saw that her belly wasn't swollen any more. They watched Devaki for a few days then the eunuch reported to Kans. "Milord, it seems Devaki has aborted the foetus."

Kans scowled at them, "How did this happen when you were there to watch?"

"It must have happened late at night," the eunuch offered as an explanation.

"The foetus must have been scared of me!" Kans laughed and dismissed the man. If the baby was not born, there was no cause to worry, he reasoned.

In due course of time Rohini gave birth to a robust boy in Gokul village. Vasudev and Devaki were delighted to receive the news. Kans also came to know but did not worry as it was not Devaki's child.

On the eighth occasion the Lord of Elysium himself alighted in Vasudev's abode and rested in Devaki's womb. As before, Kans received the news from the maids and warned them to watch Devaki closely.

As her pregnancy progressed, Devaki said to Vasudev, "Would you like to call Rohini?"

"No, Devaki. We should not try that again," Vasudev replied. "If Rohini comes here, becomes pregnant and you lose your child again, Kans will certainly get suspicious. He must have received news of Rohini giving birth to a son. We are lucky that he hasn't killed him. But if the same story repeats, he is bound to see the connection."

They kept on worrying, trying to think of a solution, but couldn't come up with any. Around this time they received news that Chief Nand's wife Yashoda was also pregnant in the village of Gokul. Unknown to them the Demigoddess of Sleep had embarked on her assignment.

When Devaki entered the seventh month of pregnancy monsoon arrived in the land. Cool breeze took away the suffocating heat that had smothered people for preceding months. The earth joyfully received the showers and turned green with burgeoning vegetation. Light rain soon gave way to dark clusters of cloud. By the time Devaki entered the ninth month heavy rains lashed Mathura.

On the eighth night of the dark fortnight of the last month of monsoons, the sky turned very dark. Lightning streaked the sky with thunder as Devaki went into labour.

"It's your turn to get into act now," at that opportune moment the Great Lord ordered the Deity of Sleep. Reclining in her cosy bed within Yashoda's belly, she cast a sleep spell on the land. The servants and sentries in Vasudev's mansion fell into an uncontrollable slumber.

At the stroke of midnight both Devaki in Mathura city and Yashoda in Gokul village gave birth to children, the former to a boy and the latter to a girl.

"Kans will be here soon now," Devaki, shaking in fear asked Vasudev, "what shall we do?"

"I have been thinking. The maids and guards are asleep,"

Vasudev replied, "I will take the baby to Gokul and ask Chief Nand to hide him. He can send him to the cowherds of the forests."

"But what shall we tell Kans? He is bound to ask us."

"I will tell him it was stillborn and I buried it." Vasudev replied.

"Will he believe that?"

"Most probably not."

"Then?"

"He might torture me to show the place where I buried it," Vasudev's face was set in determination. "I will bear it for the sake of the child."

"So shall I. Let's hurry now..." Devaki said with equal determination.

Vasudev took a wicker basket and lined its bottom with folds of soft cloth. Devaki kissed the baby. As Vasudev put the baby in the basket, they were astonished to notice it smile faintly. The baby was of dusky complexion, and it radiated a pleasant aura as it lay happily in the basket.

"Take care and return quickly," Devaki whispered as she helped lift the basket and put it on Vasudev's head. He held a stout stick in his hand and left the mansion. There was a lull in the rain when he stepped out. Walking quickly and supporting himself with the staff, he took care not to slip and fall in the slush. Within a short time he reached the Yamuna River. Periodic lightning showed him the way. The swollen current was quite strong. The water was dark with bubbles of foam flowing swiftly on the surface. Vasudev stepped in the water carefully resting his weight on the stick. He felt the current pushing him in its direction, but walked on with determination. The water level rose steadily, from knee to thigh, waist and shoulders as he progressed. At that point it started raining again. He had covered the baby with thick cloth, but was worried it would get wet. Unknown to him a large cobra floating in the current took shelter in the basket and as it spread its vast hood the child was protected under it from the rain. By the time Vasudev reached midstream the water rose above his shoulders. He shuddered with the thought that he would drown and the baby with him. Suddenly he noticed that the water had started subsiding. What he did not know was that the baby's foot sticking out of the basket had touched the water with its toe. Instantly, the rain subsided and the cobra slithered away.

Vasudev reached the other bank. He was pressed for time, for he feared Kans could arrive at the mansion any time. He hurried up the slope. He knew the path to Gokul village which was not far from the river. Chief Nand's house was located in the centre of the village. The village was quiet. Even dogs did not bark as they were all asleep under the spell of the goddess.

He reached the Chief's house and called out to his friend softly. There was no reply. The door swung open at his touch. He crossed the outer room illuminated by a lamp burning on the mantle. In the room inside he saw Nand's wife Yashoda on a bed and the midwife slumped on the floor in a slumber. The new born baby girl lay in a cradle beside. As he put the basket down, the Lord inside the basket and the Deity in the cradle smiled at each other.

Nand was nowhere to be seen. He was asleep in another room. Vasudev had planned to entrust his son to him and leave, but as he saw the baby girl, a thought occurred to him. What if he exchanged the babies? May be if Kans saw that it was a mere girl, he would not harm her! No sooner the thought occurred, he quickly exchanged the babies. He had no time to waste. He did not wait a moment more. He picked up the basket and retraced his steps.

Vasudev's return passage was uneventful. He was back within an hour. When he returned to the mansion he saw the guards still nodding at their stations. He entered the dark building quietly. Devaki was surprised to see him bring the baby back in the basket. She was relieved as Vasudev explained to her his action while he changed his wet clothes.

"I hope the brute spares the poor girl," she said as she took the baby and held her to her bosom.

A few minutes after Vasudev's arrival, the maids woke up from their stupor. They saw the baby and rushed to inform the sentries, who were also waking up. One of them dashed off to inform Kans, who was in a restless sleep in his bed. He arrived at the mansion, swaggering along the corridor and entered Devaki's room.

"What have we here?" he looked curiously at the baby.

"A girl!"

"My dear brother, what harm can a mere girl do to you?" Devaki pleaded in a humble tone.

"Hmm..." Kans thought as he stroked his moustache. "The female baby of a snake is still a snake! Can't take a chance!" he declared.

"Please! Spare her, please!" Devaki clutched the girl close to her chest.

Vasudev was horrified that he had been instrumental in the death of his friend's daughter. He lunged forward to prevent Kans, but the guards held him back. Kans pulled the baby away from Devaki's hands forcefully. He raised it above his head to hurl it, when the girl slipped out of his grip. She floated out of his reach and chuckled in glee. The sound of the baby's guffaw sent a chill down the spines of those who saw the spectacle.

"Lo! Your nemesis eludes you!" She said in a grownup voice, and swiftly flew away through the window waving its tiny arms. She soared high up in the sky and dived straight to the appointed station in Vindhya Mountains where she appeared in her new shining form of a goddess.

The people in Vasudev's mansion stood rooted to the spot as they watched the miracle unfold. Kans sank to his knees and beat his chest.

"All my efforts have gone in vain! The baby has escaped! I have been defeated!" he lamented. He got up slowly and went away with his head bent low.

Devaki and Vasudev embraced, laughing and crying at the same time, unable to believe that they had managed to save their son without harming the daughter of their friend.

3. Growing up in Gokul

As the effect of the slumber-spell wore off, Chief Nand and his wife Yashoda woke up, as did the midwife, in their house in Gokul village. Yashoda looked at the cradle and saw the beautiful, dark baby radiating bliss. She paused for a brief moment wondering if it was a boy or girl she had given birth to. The midwife too was confused. But they were so enchanted by its beauty, they thought no more. Nand entered the room, rubbing sleep out of his eyes. His eyes lit up the moment they rested on the baby.

The first to visit the new mother was Vasudev's elder wife Rohini and her one year old son. The boy had been named Balram. He was fascinated by the baby and wanted to hold it. Women from the neighbourhood, known as Gopis, sparing time from their daily chores, visited the Chief's wife. Soon the word of the cute baby spread and over the morning, Gopas and Gopis from the entire village came to take a look.

In his palace in Mathura, Kans pondered over the previous night's happening and wondered about the baby girl's words, "Your nemesis eludes you," she had said. Did it mean the girl was his nemesis? Or did it mean that Devaki's eighth child had somehow escaped? Yet, how could that be? The guards and servants were trusted.

"Depute all your spies and find out how many babies were born in and around Mathura last night," he ordered the captain of his elite force. By evening he had the report. Two babies were born the previous night. First was Devaki's daughter, second was a boy in the Chief's house in Gokul village across the river.

Should he send soldiers and have the baby killed? He pondered. This might lead to open rebellion, he thought. He had reports of much displeasure among citizens against his action of killing Devaki's babies. But that was within the family. Now if he terminated babies at random, the Vrishni tribe would not tolerate it. Chief Nand was a popular and prominent leader of the Vrishnis. At last Kans sent for the wet nurse who had breastfed him in his childhood. He shared a bond with her and trusted her.

"I have a special task for you," he told the attractive, middle-aged, buxom woman.

"I will do anything for you, milord," she replied with a toothy smile.

"There is a baby whom I want you to nurse. You will do it quietly and apply this sweet-tasting poison to your nipples while you do it." He handed her a bottle. He ordered the spy to give her details of the baby's house.

The nurse arrived in Gokul towards noon. She scouted the Chief's house located in a lush plot of land, encircling it from afar. Hiding behind a large tree, she saw the visitors to the house leave by lunch hour. Taking cover behind flowering shrubs, she approached the house and entered the large cowshed behind it. She looked in through a window and saw Chief Nand and his wife taking their midday meal in the kitchen. The baby was in a cradle in a room nearby.

She entered the house on tiptoe and looked at the baby. She was astonished that a day-old baby could actually smile, or was it her imagination? She picked up the baby, happy that it did not cry and draw attention of the parents in the other room. She carried it to the garden and sat behind a clump of shrubs. Quickly she applied the poison to her bosom and started feeding the baby. The boy suckled happily making guttural sounds. She experienced a queer sensation as he continued sucking even after the flow of milk ceased. She tried to push the baby away, but he held her fast. She felt an excruciating pain in her chest and tried to drop the baby from her arms, but couldn't. She collapsed and writhed in agony as she felt the very life being drawn away from her heart. In a few moments she gave up the ghost as she let out a long scream.

Yashoda and Nand were alarmed by her cry and rushed to the cradle. They were dismayed to see the cradle empty. Nand ran into the garden from where the cry had come. Yashoda was on his heels. They saw the body of the woman with the baby in her arms. The woman's breast had turned blue from the poison, but the baby seemed safe enough. Yashoda picked it up in a hurry, showering kisses on it.

Gopas from nearby arrived as they heard the shouts. The incident caused some commotion in the village. By evening the news reached Mathura and Kans. Kans was perplexed. How did the nurse die? Was it an accident or a heart-attack? Or was the baby responsible in some way? He started thinking of more ways to eliminate the baby while he continued holding Vasudev and Devaki under house confinement for fear that the couple might bear more children.

After twelve days had passed, Nand organized a grand naming ceremony for the child. Entire Gokul village assembled at the Chief's place. The place was decorated with colourful flags and banners, and the cradle with toys and balloons. The horns of cows were painted and sported ribbons. There was food and drink, music and dance. Yashoda, Rohini and the Gopis sang. With the prescribed rites, the boy was named Krishna for he was of dark complexion.

Child Krishna was adored by all villagers, especially the Gopis of Gokul. They treated him with added adulation after he had done away with his assailant, the poison woman. He grew up among the Gopa children along with his elder brother Balram.

He crawled to the cow pens and played with calves with their large black eyes and shiny skins. As a toddler he would never sit at one place and wandered all over the Chief's house and garden. Yashoda was concerned he would hurt himself. One day she found him peeping into the well in the yard and was alarmed.

"You are such a naughty child," she chided, "You always worry mama, don't you?" Krishna's reply was a toothless grin.

In exasperation she fastened him to a heavy stone mortar with a piece of rope around his waist. The mortar was as high as the child, so feeling secure that this would keep him away from wandering, she continued with her chores. As she went out of sight, Krishna started crawling, dragging with ease the heavy implement behind him. He crawled across the yard and into the adjoining grove. As he passed between two saplings growing close to each other, the mortar got stuck between them. He pulled and the trees were uprooted. He continued dragging them behind him. He crossed the grove and crawled into the street. Gopas and Gopis thronged to see the spectacle, astonished at the child's strength. Yashoda heard the commotion outside and rushed to the street.

As he grew Krishna developed a taste for butter. He would not touch his food unless butter was also on the plate. Yashoda was worried he would get fat and tried to ration it. Krishna would sneak into the kitchen while she was busy and steal it.

One evening when Chief Nand returned from the pastures, Yashoda rushed to him.

"I have something to tell you," she gushed, "today I caught Krishna quietly coming out of the kitchen. I suspected he had stolen butter and started scolding him."

"So what's new in this?" he said.

"Hear me out, please. When Krishna denied having eaten butter, I asked him to open his mouth. I looked into his mouth and saw thousands of stars, suns and galaxies. I saw the entire universe in all its splendour in his buccal cavity."

"You know what," Nand said in wonderment, "I am convinced this boy is no ordinary child. We are uncommonly blessed to have him amongst us."

As they grew, the two agnate brothers Krishna and Balram became quite attached to each other.

"Let's go to the river," Krishna would tell Balram.

They loved the Yamuna and the woods on its banks. They were a sight to watch together. Krishna was dark, lean and lithe with curly black hair, while Balram, the older of the two, was fair, and brawny with dark brown hair. Krishna liked to dress in cream attire while Balram loved blue. Krishna always had a peacock feather stuck in the headband. Krishna led all activities and Balram remained a supporter in the background.

Days on end they wandered the grasslands dotted with scenic spots bordering the Yamuna. Together they played with the cowherd children while they grazed the dappled cattle. They went to the nearby forest and climbed trees. They played games, hanging from the branches and leaping onto the ground.

"Who wants to have butter?" Krishna asked the group

one day.

"Me!" Many hands went up.

"Then we have to find it first."

"I saw the pp... priest's wife ch... churn lots of curds," a shy boy named Sudama volunteered.

"Did you see properly, you nitwit?" Some of the group laughed at his stutter.

"Don't anyone dare laugh at him!" Krishna supported the fellow. "The priest's wife is probably preparing for the forthcoming temple feast. Tonight after everyone is asleep let's gather behind the priest's place."

That night Krishna led the boys in a raid on the temple kitchen. He made Sudama stand near the door as a lookout. Sudama was very happy to be trusted with the important job. Krishna quietly entered the kitchen through a window, picked up the large earthen pot of butter and handed over to Balram. The Gopa boys made good with the butter. Sitting in the atrium of the temple, Krishna distributed the butter equally among them.

When the Gopis found out that the boys were on a rampage, they complained to Yashoda. She advised them to follow her suit and hang the pots of butter and curds out of reach of the boys in slings from the ceiling. Next time Krishna's gang entered the kitchen of the village scribe, they found the pots hung high up.

"What s...shall we do now, K...Krishna?" Sudama asked.

"Balram, you crouch below the pots," Krishna quickly devised a tactic to overcome the problem, "Sudama, you climb on his shoulders." He gave Sudama a hand. Then Krishna, supported by other Gopas, stood atop Sudama's shoulders and as a sturdy Balram stood up to his full height, Krishna reached the pots.

"Your son is too much," that evening too, Gopis whose kitchens had been raided, came to the Chief's house to complain to Yashoda.

Next afternoon when the Gopis came to the river to bathe, wash clothes and fetch water, Krishna, hiding behind a tree, chose the complainants and broke their earthen pots with well-aimed pebbles from a sling. He snatched the set of dry clothes they kept on the bank when they entered the river to bathe and would not return these until they begged and promised not to complain against him.

Yet the Gopis adored the naughty boy. They developed a love-hate relation with him. They loved listening to Krishna playing flute in the nearby grove. They wove garlands of flowers and offered them to Krishna. The Gopas and Gopis spent many an afternoon in the grove dancing in a circle with Krishna playing in the centre. The Gopis vied with each other to dance with Krishna. The enchanting music that Krishna made attracted birds and animals as it did the humans. The cows and calves that the Gopas brought to the water were fascinated by the divine music and formed the outermost ring of the circle.

One afternoon as Krishna arrived at their favourite spot on the river bank, he found a young Gopi sitting below a tree all by herself. She looked up as he approached her. Her large, black eyes seemed sad.

"What's the matter?" he asked, "Tell me what troubles you."

She shook her head, reluctant to open up.

"S...She hails from a...another village across the r...river," Sudama volunteered.

Krishna found out her name was Radha, who was married into Nand village recently. He realized she felt lonely here.

"Welcome to our dear little Nand village," he smiled. "Come, dance with me!"

He took her hand gently. The shy girl took hesitant steps with him as the group danced. Soon, she opened up and warmed to him.

"I felt so lonely in this new place," she confided in him when they met next time in the grove. "My husband is a nice man, but dominated by his mother."

They sat on the soft grass and chatted. She was older than Krishna, yet she found a friend and confidante in Krishna. He became a kindred spirit for her in this new place. She could hardly wait for an opportunity to visit the river and meet Krishna. They spent long afternoons nestled on swings hung from tall trees.

"Your wife is always at the river," her mother-in-law complained to her husband. "She adores that son of Yashoda."

"I don't mind if she joins the Gopa dance once in a while,"

Radha's husband said. "But she should finish her daily chores, first." They failed to understand the platonic relation Radha shared with Krishna.

Krishna arranged music and dance in the meadows on moonlit nights of autumn. The Gopas and Gopis loved those occasions. Radha sneaked out of her house after everyone was asleep and joined the dances. Radha danced with Krishna lacing fingers together. They sat watching the moon reflected in the Yamuna and talked for hours, which made other Gopis jealous.

When spring set in Gokul, on the day after the full moon, Krishna and his band of Gopas sprayed coloured water on each other through pumps made of hollow bamboo. They roamed the streets of the village snaring unsuspecting Gopis and doused them in colour.

"Eeep!" The Gopis shrieked and ran in mock alarm but they loved the sport. Radha would invariably dress in white that day, so Krishna could drench her in many colours.

It became an annual feature and the Gopas gathered in the village square on the particular day and splashed colour on each other. They danced and feasted the whole day.

4. Valor in Vraj

Back in Mathura, Vasudev and Devaki, under confinement in their home, periodically received news of Krishna and Balram's progress from some of the servants who had earned their trust. They felt happy that these two had escaped from Kans and hoped that they would someday put an end to his unjust rule.

Kans also received regular updates of the lad and his charm. He had some friends among the demonic clans. He induced one of them to visit Nand village and kill Krishna.

The demon arrived in Nand one afternoon. He found the Gopas playing leapfrog in the grove. He took the form of a Gopa boy and joined them. He wanted to team with Krishna, but when lots were drawn he had to become Balram's partner. In the course of the game, the players had to carry their partners on their shoulders and run to a vast banyan tree. When it was the demon's turn he picked up Balram, but instead of running towards the tree he started carrying him off in the opposite direction. Perched atop his shoulders, a confused Balram looked at Krishna.

"Remember your power," Krishna shouted.

Balram was muscular and heavy of weight. The demon in the boy's shape, as he tried to make off, was unable to bear Balram's burden. He gave up the human form and assumed his huge demonic form. His skin turned hairy and eyes red. He tried to throw Balram down but Balram held firm with his knees. He hit the demon with his hammer-like fists and cracked the demon's skull, who fell down and breathed his last. The Gopas were astonished at Balram's strength. The elders suspected that Kans was behind the demon's mission to hurt the boys, but they were unable to do anything about it.

In the following years Kans made two more attempts. He sent a demon who took the shape of a fierce bull, attacked the Gopas and caused havoc in Nand village. Krishna took him by the horns and eliminated him after a terrifying bull fight. Then Kans sent another demon who took the form of a wild horse, who kicked and bit Krishna but was slain too.

"Check and tell me if the Gopas of Nand village are paying taxes regularly," Kans called his head of tax collectors.

"Yes, milord, they are fairly regular."

"We need more milk for the citizens of Mathura," Kans instructed, "have a notice sent to the Gopas that they must send all their milk produce to Mathura."

The Gopas were quite unhappy over these orders.

"Kans' men are not allowing us to keep enough milk for children and calves," they complained to Chief Nand. Krishna and his friends were affected for there was no butter left in Gokul to steal. There was great resentment against Kans among the Gopas.

When summer came to the land, the pastures turned brown. The river dried up. The Gopa council met to discuss the lack of fodder for cattle. Krishna, now sixteen, was invited to the meeting.

"Our cattle have grazed the land dry around Gokul village. The Gopas have cut down trees for timber and turned the woods into barren moors," he said. "The ancestors owned a land called Vraj up north along the river, but the Gopas have forgotten about it. The river has many lakes and ponds in its course there. There are pleasant woods. The hills are covered with thick forests. I suggest we shift our habitation from Gokul to Vraj and reclaim it."

The Gopas deliberated and took the decision to move their habitation. Over the next few days, they packed all their belongings on carts and led their herds to Vraj, where they settled on the vast land overlooking the Yamuna.

The Gopas were very happy in the new place lush with verdure. There were enough patches of grassland to graze the cattle. Nearby were hills known as Govardhan on which grew thick forests that housed all sorts of wildlife. The Gopas harvested fruits and bountiful produce that the forests yielded.

Krishna's band of youths roamed along the river exploring new spots to sport. At some distance from their new settlement they came across a dark pool in the course of the river. No trees grew near it and no birds flew over the water. There were skeletons of animals scattered along the banks. Perched on a rock that overhung the water, Sudama dropped some pebbles in the water. Judging from the bubbles that rose to the surface, Krishna concluded that the water ran very deep.

"What are you guys doing here?" An old Gopa asked them. He was gathering kindling from the thicket and carried a bundle of firewood on his head.

"We want to go for a swim in the pool," Balram replied.

"Are you crazy?" The man seemed shocked.

"Why, what's the matter?" Krishna asked.

"Don't you know? This is Kalia's lake!"

"And w...who might K...Kalia be?" Sudama asked.

"Kalia? He is the serpent king of this region. He has not one, but five hoods. He stays with his family in this lake fed by the Yamuna. He has terrorized the people in the region. He devours everyone and anyone who comes nearby. Even birds are scared to fly over the lake for he can leap out of the water and snap them. Go home, you shouldn't be here."

"It's Kalia who shouldn't be here," Krishna said. "The land belongs to the Gopas. Our cattle need to graze and drink here."

Krishna girdled his loins and without warning he dived into the dark lake, while the old man watched in alarm. His friends were aghast. Krishna swam around the lake smiling up at them. Several serpents surfaced around him. They hissed and attacked Krishna, but he remained smiling. Their bites did not affect him. He picked them and hurled them away.

Sudama and some of the friends were shaken. Some of them bolted to the village to inform Yashoda and the Chief.

Presently, turbulence occurred in the centre of the lake. Five enormous hoods appeared amongst great coils. The monster Kalia had blazing eyes and his five tongues flicked menacingly. He swam swiftly towards Krishna and enveloped him in the coils of his thick, long body, trying to suffocate him.

Balram watched quietly as Krishna slipped through the binding coils. He scaled Kalia's hoods and stood on the central hood. He held the tail of the serpent in one hand and danced on his hoods. Kalia writhed violently but could not dislodge Krishna. The drama went on for some time.

Yashoda and Nand arrived in haste along with several

Gopas in tow. They were amazed at the sight of Krishna laughing and dancing atop Kalia's hoods while the serpent cried in agony. Two women, half serpent down the waist, appeared in front of Krishna with folded hands. They were Kalia's wives.

"Please take mercy on our lord," they pleaded humbly, "please don't kill him."

"Let him promise to leave this land," Krishna replied.

Kalia assumed a half human form and submitted meekly. "I shall not bother the men and animals here. I shall leave the lake, my lord. Please tell me where I should reside?"

"Go to the middle of the ocean with your family and courtiers, and live there in peace."

As Kalia and his followers left along the down current of Yamuna, the lake waters turned clear as crystal. The Gopas rejoiced while Yashoda embraced her son.

That year as the Gopas prepared for the festival to worship Indra the rain god, Krishna asked his father, "Why do we have to worship Indra?"

"It's because of him we enjoy abundance on earth, son."

"I think it's the hills of Govardhan that afford us all that we desire," Krishna said thoughtfully, "The woods offer us fruit, and the pastures offer grass for our cattle, the streams that originate in the mountain feed the river and give us water. We should be worshipping the mountain, not Indra."

"If we do that, Indra will be displeased with us," some of the elder Gopas opined.

"What kind of god gets angry and troubles people? Isn't it the god's duty to love and protect people? Don't worry. The mountain is our refuge, it will protect us," Krishna replied.

They argued back and forth. At last the Gopas accepted Krishna's contention and decided to worship Mount Govardhan. The Gopas and Gopis made preparations and went up the hills. They worshipped the mountain with offerings of curds and butter. They sang in praise of the mount. The festivities lasted for three days.

In his capital in Svarg, the lower echelon of Elysium, Indra, the god of rains, turned angry on hearing that the Gopas had given up his worship.

"I shall smite them with my lightning weapon," he thought.

He ordered dark clouds to assemble over Vraj. Goaded by Indra, floating in from the seas, the clouds heavy with rain crowded the skies and shrouded the sun. The land of Vraj trembled with the sound of thunder and the crash of lightning. The hill side collapsed as beams of lightning struck. Water, carrying quantities of mud, rushed down the hills and the Yamuna swelled engulfing everything on its banks. The fields sank under the deluge. In the beginning people retreated to their houses. But the wind blew away roofs of houses and cow sheds. Cows mooed in terror and wild-eyed calves, shivering in the cold, stuck to their mothers. The Gopas ran crouching under the pelting rain and assembled at Chief Nand's.

"Where is your son who said he will protect us from Indra's wrath?" some of them demanded. "Ask him to beg for forgiveness from Lord Indra now, before it is too late."

Krishna, unaffected by the calamity, faced them calmly. He merely said, "Let's go up to Mount Govardhan, it will protect us."

Through the blinding showers he led all the living beings to the foot of the mountain. His friends formed teams and guided people and cattle in an organized way through the murky streams.

Krishna stood quietly facing the mount. He shut his eyes for a brief moment and summoning his strength assumed a form like the mountain. He lifted the mountain with his hands. For a moment the mountain shifted and shook wildly. Trees and rocks slid down the slopes. Tigers roared in their caves in the hills. Birds left their nests and took to the sky, but because their wings were wet, many of them fell down. Exercising his immense strength, Krishna steadied the mountain and held it high above his head. He asked the Gopas to take shelter underneath. They supported the mountainous roof with columns of hard timber. The people, their carts and herds of Vraj entered the safe space beneath the vast, impregnable umbrella. The cows mooed happily while clouds roared outside in frustration. Govardhan stood glorious in Krishna's upraised hands with clouds swirling around it. Rain washed off harmlessly from the sides of the mountain. All of Indra's efforts were fruitless as the men and animals found safety.

Seven nights passed, but Indra could not overcome the Gopas. On the eighth morning the wind died down, clouds dispersed and the sun shone again on the land of Gopas. Swan flew over their favourite spots on the Yamuna. The Gopas came out from under the shelter and Krishna placed the mountain down. Vraj returned to normalcy. Indra arrived on his famed white elephant and approached Krishna in all humility. "I had forgotten who you are, Great Lord," he said. Krishna smiled and there was peace in Vraj.

5. Triumph in Mathura

As Krishna grew up in Gokul, Kans was worried. By now he was almost certain that Krishna was Vasudev's eighth son who had escaped from him. He reasoned that Vasudev had somehow managed to switch the babies. He also realized that he had a formidable opponent in Krishna. After the attempts by his wet-nurse and the three demons had failed, he decided to handle the situation with more cunning.

One afternoon he visited Vasudev and Devaki at their place along with some leaders from the various Yadav tribes.

"I hear your son is growing and doing well in Gokul village," he began in a conciliatory tone. "I wish to honour him." Those present realized he appeared to be alluding to Balram as son, but meant Krishna.

"All you elders and seniors of the Yadavs are honourable and guide me in ruling," Kans eulogized the Yadav chiefs. "You are all great archers and acquainted with the scriptures. You have knowledge of the art of governance.

"I plan to perform a bow ceremony soon." Kans continued, "I have acquired a strong and excellent bow and will take possession of it in this ceremony. Let us honour the youths from Gokul on this occasion." Kans turned to Akrur, one of the tribal chiefs, who was also a friend of Chief Nand and Vasudev. "Go speedily to Gokul and invite Balram, and yes, also Krishna. I hear they are valorous and they need to be felicitated. Invite all the senior Gopas and their Chief Nand too."

Kans left Vasudev's house with the chiefs and went to his palace, pleased with himself thinking his subterfuge was successful. He thought of ways to deal with Krishna and Balram when they arrived in Mathura. He had a prize elephant of ill temper and had turned a man-killer. He had two wrestlers who hailed from far south and were of demonic origin. They were highly skilled in their art and had defeated every wrestler in Aryavart. No one could blame him for hurting Chief Nand's boy if he accepted a challenge from the wrestlers and was killed. He waited patiently for Krishna to arrive.

When Kans' counsellor Akrur arrived in Gokul that evening, he was welcomed by Chief Nand as he was a long time friend. He offered him sweets and milk and they sat in the village office and chatted with senior Gopas. Presently Krishna and Balram along with the other cowherds returned with the cows from the pastures and joined them.

"King Kans wants to honour your sons," Akrur informed then when they were all together. "He has also invited all the senior Gopas to Mathura."

Nand was surprised at the King's gesture. Although he did not reveal it, he was suspicious of Kans' sudden generosity. However, Krishna received the news with much pleasure.

"I have wanted to go to Mathura for so long," he said in obvious delight.

"Me too," Balram joined him.

Their Gopa friends were excited at the prospect of seeing the city. That night the Gopas made preparations to leave for Mathura in the morning.

When Nand had an opportunity, he took Krishna aside and spoke to him in a hushed tone.

"You are eighteen now, so I can tell you a secret. You are aware that Kans has usurped power from his father the old king Ugrasen, and put him under house arrest. Have you wondered how a son could do this to his father? It is because there is a secret behind Kans' birth, which only some of the senior Yadavs know. Once, before Kans was born, his mother, the queen of Ugrasen, had gone for a picnic with other royal women. While sporting in the scenic woods, she lost her way. Alone she wandered seeking to go back to the group, when a demon saw her. He took the form of Ugrasen and made love to her on the banks of the lake. Somehow, she realized that he was not Ugrasen for his manners were different. When she questioned him, he revealed his original self and laughed at her.

"This child, Kans, was born by deceit from the seed of a demon. He is not the son of the gentle and honest King Ugrasen. You must not trust him. I have doubts of his real intention in inviting you to Mathura."

"Thank you for cautioning me, but I am not afraid of Kans," Krishna smiled at the Chief.

*

Early in the morning Krishna and Balram left for Mathura in minister Akrur's chariot. The entire village gathered and bid him farewell with a sad heart. Chief Nand and other Gopas followed him in bullock carts. As the chariot was nearing the Yamuna, a figure stepped out of the trees onto the shadowed path. It was Radha. Akrur halted the chariot and Krishna leaped out and went to her.

"Farewell my friend," she said in a choked voice, "I understand you have great things in store for you. You cannot live the life of a cowherd forever."

He wiped her tears and gave her his flute as a souvenir of their friendship. This was their last meeting. They smiled at each other, yet tears welled up in their eyes. Their friendship, along with the mirabilia Krishna performed in Gokul, became a legend in the land.

When they reached Mathura the brothers stayed at Akrur's house. Their Gopa friends arrived too and stayed in a lodge for travellers. Towards evening Krishna and Balram sought the minister's permission to take a look at the city.

"Do see the sites here," Akrur said, "but be careful not to go near Vasudev's house."

"Why? He is Balram's father..." Krishna was surprised.

"The king suspects that you are also his eighth son," Akrur replied.

"Really? This is curious. Tell us in detail," Krishna urged him, pretending to be unaware of it.

On his insistence Akrur revealed them all about the prophecy of Devaki's eighth son and why Kans thought Krishna was the one destined to obliterate him. The two brothers listened with attention.

"Kans is highly inimical to Vasudev," Akrur concluded. "That is why I ask you not to visit Vasudev, before you have met the king."

They promised not to go to Vasudev's place and went to see the city. Along with their young friends from the village they roamed the roads lined with elegant mansions and delightful parks. Presently they came to the market place. They saw colourful garlands being sold in one place.

"Give us some garlands," they told the vendor, "we are going to see the king tomorrow."

The garland seller offered them some with a smile and Krishna blessed him.

Further down the street they saw a hunchback woman carrying sandal paste and scented unguents.

"Give us some sandal paste," they asked her, "we are going to see the king tomorrow."

"Why, sure," She smiled at the handsome lads, "let me apply it on your forehead."

"Why do you walk with a crouch?" Krishna touched her back gently.

"I was born a hunchback, that is why."

"I don't think so, try to walk straight," he urged, patting her on the back.

She tried to straighten herself and was amazed to find that the hunch on her back had disappeared.

"You are a performer of miracles," she said, "I have fallen in love with you."

Krishna smiled, the Gopas laughed and they proceeded down the market lane. They saw a laundry with many coloured silk garments put out to dry.

"Give us some garments," Krishna asked the owner.

"You rustic folks, you smell of cow dung," the washer man looked them over with disdain. "These clothes belong to the king."

"We are going to meet the king tomorrow. That is why we ask."

"Get lost or I will smite you, you beggars," he raised his staff.

Balram held his staff-wielding hand in a powerful grip and the man couldn't move a finger. Krishna chose some decent clothes for him and Balram, as the man watched helplessly. When they left, the man went to the captain and lodged a complaint.

Presently they reached the building where the new bow was stored for next day's ceremony. They requested the guards to take a look at the bow. It was made of the best of steels and rested on its velvet bed. Before the guards could object, Krishna lifted the bow and tried to string it. The bow snapped in two in Krishna's hands. The guards were aghast. They rushed to the captain to report the incident, and he immediately went to see Kans.

"Some insolent cowherds from Gokul have broken the bow meant for tomorrow's ceremony, sire," he reported, "and they have also robbed your garments from the laundry."

"Hmm," Kans said, "I know who those cowherds are."

He treated the breaking of the bow as a bad omen. He felt fear grip his heart. This really must be the eighth son of Devaki, he thought. He sent for the two wrestlers and the elephant rider.

"Keep your mount hungry tonight. Feed liquor and intoxicants early tomorrow. Let him be inebriated and enraged." Kans instructed the mahout. "Station the elephant at the entrance of the stadium where I am going to meet Vasudev's sons. Goad the elephant as soon as you see them. Let the beast trample on them as they arrive."

He turned to the two wrestlers. "Tomorrow will be the test of your skill. You must deal with the two cowherd youths from Gokul. Don't show any mercy on them. They must not leave the arena alive." He handed them bags of gold coins. "There will be more when you have accomplished the task."

Early next morning Krishna and Balram donned the new garments and wore garlands. They smeared their arms with the sandal paste. Krishna stuck a peacock feather in his head band. They left for the stadium along with the Gopas and Akrur.

When they approached the gates of the arena, the mahout goaded the boozed up elephant. It took a few steps towards Krishna and then paused. It raised its trunk in a salute and let out a cheerful trumpet. The rider was left aghast, but couldn't get the elephant to attack. Krishna gently patted the pachyderm on its trunk and crossed the gates.

With a smile Krishna and Balram entered the arena lined with stands on which the citizens of Mathura were seated. The place was decorated with colourful hangings and the ground was prepared by sprinkling water by watermen with leather tanks strapped to their backs. The entire city of Mathura was present there, eager to look at the cowherd who had broken the royal bow. Kans was seated on his throne in a brightly canopied stand. His two wives, the twin daughters of Jarasandh, were in another pavilion close by. Kans had particularly invited Vasudev and Devaki so they could witness their son's death. They were seated among the Yadav chiefs. Akrur went to the officers' stands and Chief Nand along with the Gopas took seats among the crowd.

As Krishna started walking towards the throne, the two wrestlers advanced.

"Lo cowherd, I hear you defeated some bull and a horse," the taller of the two challenged Krishna, "Can you take on a real wrestler?"

"You look formidable sire, but I can certainly try if the King permits," Krishna said with exaggerated humility. Kans laughed at that and raised his hand granting his permission.

The broader wrestler challenged Balram. The brothers girded their loins and got ready for the bout. Krishna and the wrestler clasped each other's hands in salutation. The moment the man released his hand, Krishna grabbed it again and in a lightening move pulled him. The wrestler landed on his knees. Krishna quickly circled him and caught him by the shoulders from behind. He lifted the opponent and threw him down. Surprised at the boy's strength, the man shook his head and gathered himself. He advanced again with outstretched arms, but with more caution. Quickly Krishna crouched and rushed to get between his legs. He lifted the heavyweight and threw him backwards over his shoulder. The man landed with a thud that shook the ground. Before he could get up, Krishna was on top of him and placed a foot on the man's chest, as he stood smiling. The wrestler realized that he was no match to the opponent. He conceded defeat. Krishna looked at Balram who too had done short work of the other wrestler.

They went towards Kans, whose face had turned red with wrath.

"Kill these cowherds," he screamed at his guards, "...and that conniving Vasudev too. Drive the evil cowherd chief out of my city!"

Krishna leapt on to the podium where Kans was seated even before the guards could move. He was so quick, one moment he was seen on the ground and the other next to Kans' throne. He held Kans by the scruff of his neck. Kans' crown fell and clattered down the steps. Kans looked into Krishna's eyes and was so terrified, he could not move a muscle. He realized his end was near. Holding him by his throat, Krishna dragged Kans down the steps of the stand. He threw Kans on the ground and dealt a single blow to his chest. Blood and froth welled up from Kans' mouth as he gave up his ghost.

For a moment the stadium fell silent, then realizing that they were free of the tyrant, the citizens of Mathura rejoiced, cheering Krishna and Balram. Leaving her seat in the stands Devaki, the end of her sari trailing behind her, rushed to her long-separated son and held him in her arms. She felt an ache in her bosom which could be relived only by clasping Krishna to her. Vasudev followed her and kissed Krishna's and Balram's foreheads. The Yadavs witnessed the heart-warming sight of the son meeting his parents for the first time in his life.

While there was reunion in Krishna's family, the dead king's wives lamented besides his body, as did his mother.

Krishna went and bowed to them, "I am sorry I am the cause of your bereavement, but believe me, there was no alternative to remedy the ills that the king was heaping on the populace."

He then addressed Kans' mother, "I would have spared his life if I could, but you know milady, he was born of a demon. Please forgive me if you can."

"Alas, no one can undo the past," the old queen replied, "I request you to arrange a proper funeral for my son."

"Of course, milady," Krishna replied, "there should be no enmity with the dead."

He turned to minister Akrur and requested him to make arrangements.

The onlookers appreciated Krishna's humbleness. All the Yadav chiefs went to Krishna. The old King Ugrasen also arrived there on hearing of Kans' death. Although grieving at his son's demise, he was also relieved that the kingdom had been freed from his clutches. He picked up the crown that had fallen and offered it to Krishna.

"You deserve to be the king of Yadavs," he said, "accept this crown and rule our land."

"No, milord," Krishna refused with a smile, "you are

the legitimate ruler of the land and after the usurper has been done away with, you must take up the position again. Our democratic traditions must be preserved." The Yadavs applauded Krishna's magnanimity.

Krishna and Balram went to live in the mansion with Vasudev and Devaki. Balram's mother Rohini also joined them from Gokul.

Next day, in a full court, Krishna ordained King Ugrasen once again as the ruler of Mathura. The citizens were very happy as were the chiefs of the various Yadav tribes.

Krishna and Balram had very little formal education while growing up in Gokul, now they had the opportunity to fulfil the desire to learn the scriptures and the essentials of governance. They along with Sudama joined the ashram of a renowned teacher called Sandipani. They adored their guru and his wife and performed all the household chore along with the other students. They ate frugal meals and collected firewood from the forests and tended to the teacher's cattle in the mornings and evenings. The day was spent in learning the Vedas, the Upanishads and other texts. At night the teacher's wife told them stories of the great Ram and how he governed his land with justice. They had a memorable stay at Sage Sandipani's ashram.

6. Destination Dwarika

When news of Kans' death reached Jarasandh in Magadh, he was enraged. He immediately set out for Mathura with his forces to avenge the death of his son-in-law. He sent messages to his allies Shishupal, prince of Chedi and Rukmi prince of Vidarbh. Like Kans, those two princes were also staunch supporters of Jarasandh and hated the Yadavs. They departed their capitals with their armies, converging on Mathura. Camping at nights those forces comprising of elephants, chariots, cavalry and infantry marched by day.

When King Ugrasen received news of the invading armies, he called a meeting of the Yadav leaders along with Krishna and Balram. The Yadavs geared up for war with Jarasandh. They ordered Mathura's gates to be closed and the city fortified. Krishna sent small detachments which constantly raided and harassed the invading armies at night while they rested and escaped before they could retaliate for they knew the land well.

The forces from Magadh and Chedi arrived and camped in the forests and grasslands surrounding Mathura waiting for Rukmi's army from Vidarbh beyond the Vindhya Mountains. The sound of bells adorning their war animals pervaded the woods as did the crunching sound of their vehicles' wheels. The land reeked with the odour of animal and human excreta. When Rukmi joined him, Jarasandh was delighted.

"Let us raze this proud Yadav city to the ground!" Jarasandh thundered. "But I want Krishna alive. I want to kill him personally for widowing my daughters!"

The combined forces of Magadh, Chedi and Vidarbh laid siege to Mathura. Mathura seemed like an island surrounded by the invaders. They shot missiles over the walls into the city and the Yadav archers retaliated from the ramparts.

The battles of missiles were followed by hand to hand fighting when King Ugrasen ordered the gates to be opened. The Yadav braves rushed out of the city. Balram led the elephant charge on Jarasandh. Krishna clashed with the forces of Shishupal from Chedi. Other Yadav chiefs took on Prince Rukmi of Vidarbh. Fierce fighting lasted for several days. The campaign dragged on beyond what Jarasandh had estimated. The Yadavs went back into the fort every night and were fortified with supplies. The invaders started running short of food, medicines and weapons as Jarasandh had attacked in rage without allowing the required time for fully preparing for the campaign.

At last Jarasandh decided to retreat. He went back to Magadh, but his ambition was further fuelled from the insult of defeat added to the hurt of his protégé being killed. He took his time to prepare for a large scale invasion. He urged several kings, whom he had subjugated before and owed allegiance to him, to join in the campaign.

The Yadavs met to discuss the threat from Jarasandh. The mood in the assembly was belligerent.

"Let us attack Jarasandh's capital Rajgriha," Balram thundered. "Offence is the best way of defence."

"Yes, I support Balram," another general joined in. "There have been eighteen skirmishes with their scouts and we have defeated them."

"I beg to differ," Krishna said when he had heard out the others. "Jarasandh is too formidable an enemy. He has ambitious friends in Shishupal and Rukmi. They are enrolling several other kings. We shall not be able to resist them, let alone attack."

"Then what is your opinion?" Balram, short-tempered as he was, asked angrily. "Should we sit like ducks for them to come and defeat us?"

"Of course not, my brother," Krishna smiled at him. "I suggest we retreat before they attack."

"What!" there were exclamations as people wondered if they had heard Krishna correctly.

"Yes, we retreat and live to fight another day," Krishna answered calmly.

"And where do you suggest we should retreat?" King Ugrasen asked.

"To the west, to the coast," Krishna said, "we should put a lot of distance between us and our enemies."

"People will call you a renegade!" Balram was aghast at Krishna's suggestion.

"Let them call me by any name, names are only a means for addressing people." Krishna smiled. "I have learned there is an island on the west coast, protected on all sides by the sea. Let us go there and create a new homeland for us. When times turn favourable, we shall reclaim Mathura."

"I think Krishna is right," at last King Ugrasen said thoughtfully. The Yadav chiefs conceded, though some of them were unhappy at the decision. It was not easy to give up the city in which their forefathers had lived for so long.

Once the decision was taken Krishna led the advance party to the west coast while the other Yadavs made preparations and followed him. Long caravans of vehicles and animals set out from Mathura for the coast. When Krishna reached the coast, he surveyed the island. It had natural protection and had forests and fresh water pools in the vicinity. To the south was Mount Raivatak.

"I want you to design a city for us," Krishna instructed Vishwakarma, the architect of the gods, after summoning him.

"This is an excellent place for a fortified city," the architect nodded, "you have chosen well. But we need more land to accommodate all your Yadav tribes. I think the lord of the sea will grant you more land if you ask him."

Krishna summoned the lord of the sea and expressed his wish. The lord conceded access and the sea receded exposing more land for the city. A large island was created for the Yadavs.

The celestial architect soon came up with a plan for a city with four gates and a harbour. There were main roads and cross roads dividing the city in eight parts. Krishna put all his men to the task of building. With the help of the celestials soon a city of unparalleled splendour emerged on the island. Multi-storeyed mansions were built for the Yadav chiefs. Spacious palaces were built for King Ugrasen, Krishna and chiefs of various Yadav tribes. There were gardens abounding with every kind of flowering plants. Tanks and ponds were located at chosen spots which abounded with the calls of rare and colourful birds. When the city was ready for occupation the celestials presented a wonderful assembly hall and placed it right in the centre of the Yadav city. The hall had columns of gold with jewels inlaid. The Yadavs were very happy to reside in their new homes. Travellers from faraway places visited the city and marvelled at its architecture. Traders in huge vessels from the lands of Mlecchaas across the ocean arrived and the city prospered. There were no beggars or poor in the city. The city was named Dwarika as it became the gate to Aryavart for travellers from overseas.

In the meanwhile enemy forces took over Mathura, but they did not chase the Yadavs to the coast as it was too far away and not all the kingdoms in the intervening lands were on friendly terms with King Jarasandh. Peace was established in the kingdoms of Aryavart as the Yadavs left Mathura and went to Dwarika, although the enmity between Jarasandh and Krishna persisted below the surface.

In the kingdom of Vidarbh beyond the Vindhya Mountains, Princess Rukmini sat on a swing on the terrace in her palace. The beautiful princess sat in the cool night under a full moon dreaming of Krishna of whom she had heard so many tales from her friends and servants. She desired to marry the dark prince of Dwarika. She often spoke to her bosom friend and wondered how this could be accomplished. However, it seemed a faraway dream as her brother Prince Rukmi was averse to the Yadavs and Krishna.

While the princess sat thinking of Krishna on the palace terrace, downstairs in the royal drawing room, her father King Bhishmak and brother Rukmi were in discussion about selecting a groom for her. Prince Rukmi was a friend of Shishupal, the King of Chedi. They had participated in Jarasandh's campaign against Mathura. Rukmi had thought of Shishupal as a prospective groom for Rukmini. Jarasandh too had thought of it as a good match.

A maid, loyal to Rukmini, overheard the King and Prince and quietly went to Rukmini's quarters.

"They are thinking of King Shishupal as groom for you, milady," she whispered to Rukmini.

"What? That vile King of Chedi?" the princess was taken aback. "Oh, what shall I do now? My dream is shattered!"

"I have thought of a way," the maid whispered, making sure that no one was in earshot. "If you send a letter to Krishna, he shall find a way."

"That's an idea!" the princess was excited. But the next moment doubts assailed her, "What can he do?"

"Leave that to him, milady," the maid assured her. "He is as intelligent as he is brave."

"But how shall I send him a letter? He is so far away..."

"My brother is a merchant's assistant, he often visits Dwarika with his master. He can deliver your letter."

Rukmini's letter arrived in Dwarika surprising Krishna. He had also heard of the princess of dazzling beauty. He consulted Balram and their friend Satyaki, another prominent warrior of the Yadavs.

"No girl should ever be married against her will," Krishna said. "She does not want to marry Shishupal, but her brother is adamant."

"Let's march on Vidarbha and rescue the princess," Balram offered a simple solution in keeping with his straightforward nature.

"It's not as easy as taking candy from a baby, my dear brother," Krishna smiled. They thought of various ways to get to Rukmini and discarded them as impractical.

Their dilemma was resolved all of a sudden when an invitation from the King of Vidarbh, Rukmini's father, arrived at Dwarika inviting King Ugrasen and the Yadavs for the nuptials of Rukmini and Shishupal. In fact, it was merely a formal invitation keeping with the protocol among royals and the Vidarbh King did not expect the Yadavs to attend considering his son's, as well as would be son-in-law's animosity with the Yadavs.

However, Krishna took the opportunity and arrived at Vidarbh with Balram and a detachment of chosen braves, a few days prior to the wedding day. They had to take the Dakshinpath or southern route which passed through the rugged Vindhya Mountains separating Vidarbh from Dwarika. The travelled on light chariots on twisting and winding roads that passed through many gorges and gullies.

"Father, why did you invite those crummy cowherds?" Rukmi fumed on hearing of the Yadavs arrival.

"Decorum has to be observed, my son," the King replied. "In politics you have to learn to say, 'nice doggy,' while you look for a stick to beat it."

The King welcomed the Yadavs formally enough but did not offer accommodation with the other royal guests. He had them reside in some buildings outside the capital well away from the parties of Jarasandh and Shishupal, least they clash and turn the wedding into a fiasco.

In the few days before the wedding, the Yadavs enjoyed the hospitality offered by the Vidarbhians. They delighted in the exquisite food and drink and partied late into the nights. Balram loved his drink a tad too much and almost forgot why he was there.

"I want you to quietly survey the territory," Krishna told his trusted friend Satyaki in private. The latter, dressed in simple clothes, went about looking at the land and studied its features. In the meanwhile the maid's brother contacted Krishna and they evolved a plan.

In the morning on the day before the wedding Rukmini visited the temple of their family deity located outside the capital city. She was accompanied by a few of her maids and guards. Krishna's men were hidden behind flowery shrubs and fountains in the garden around the temple, while he was present within the inner atrium. As soon as Rukmini stepped inside the temple, he came out from behind a pillar.

"I am Krishna," he smiled.

The princess looked at the handsome, dark prince and blushed. She had not imagined he would be so handsome. He took her hand. Outside the temple Krishna's men surrounded and tied up the guards and maids, gagging them. Krishna and Rukmini quickly mounted his chariot and left the temple precincts.

Krishna's men adept in handling horses had groomed them well and kept his horses in excellent shape. They galloped away on the hilly road to Dwarika, with the flag bearing the mark of an eagle fluttering atop. Balram and Satyaki followed them as far as the first deep ravine and halted there. They set up ambush in the ravine, by rolling down huge boulders from the hillside, which Satyaki had spotted beforehand and loosened the earth all around.

By the time someone discovered and rescued Rukmini's guards and maids, Krishna had covered much distance with

Rukmini on the way to Dwarika. There was a great uproar among the Vidarbhians, the Chedis and the Magadhs when the news of Rukmini's abduction reached them. They had gathered for a wedding, not a war. They were quite unprepared for such an eventuality. They lost some time in arranging posses to follow Krishna.

When Rukmi, Shishupal and Jarasandh reached a bend in the great gorge in the mountains, they found rocks blocking the way. They alighted from their chariots and ordered their men to move them. While the Vidarbh soldiers, lacking pickaxes and crowbars, tried to move the large obstacles manually, the Yadavs stationed high up on the two shoulders of the canyon started raining rocks and arrows. The Vidarbh troops had to fall back some distance. Balram and Satyaki, from their vantage points on opposite sides of the ravine signalled each other. They ran down the slopes to their chariots parked around the bend and galloped away towards Dwarika.

When the Yadav attack seized, the Vidarbh forces cleared the path. However, by that time the Yadavs had covered much distance. The trio was chagrined at the clever tactics of Krishna, and had to return empty handed without Rukmini. They vowed to destroy Krishna some day.

Krishna and Rukmini were wedded in a grand ceremony at Dwarika. Soon Balram also married Revati, the daughter of King Kakudmi.

7. The Jewel Thief

One morning two brothers, Prasenjeet and Satrajeet, prominent citizens of the Yadavs, showed an amazing jewel to King Ugrasen.

"Where did you find it?" Akrur, the minister, stared at the large, glittering ruby in awe.

"It was accorded by the Sun God," Prasenjeet explained. "I worship Him on the sea shore and today He appeared before me in his dazzling, golden form and rewarded me for my devotion." The two brothers were excited about their new possession.

"This jewel is known as Syamantak. Any land where this jewel resides is blessed by the Sun God," Prasen explained. "The land receives ample rainfall and abounds in crops. There is never any famine. The jewel yields riches to the possessor."

"How wonderful!" the Yadavs assembled in the court praised the jewel.

Krishna watched the Yadavs and noticed Akrur and some others eye the jewel with envy.

"I think," Krishna said, "Syamantak should be kept in the possession of King Ugrasen, for it will serve our homeland best when it is with the king."

Prasen did not like Krishna's suggestion. "The Sun God has gifted it to me. I shall not part with it." He quickly pocketed the jewel and left the assembly.

A few days after the incident King Ugrasen sent for Krishna, who promptly arrived at the court hall. He saw an agitated Satrajeet standing near the king.

"You called me, milord?" Krishna asked.

"Prasen has gone missing, Krishna," the king said. "He hasn't been seen for a couple of days now."

"Oh, is that so?" Krishna inquired, "when was he seen last?"

"He left on a hunting excursion two days ago," a visibly upset Satrajeet said. "It's not like him to stay away for so long. Normally he returns the same day."

"Why not wait for a day or two more? He might return, I guess."

"You want us to wait, so your crime can be hidden!" Satrajeet burst out.

"What do you mean?" a startled Krishna asked.

"You wanted the jewel, so you must have caused harm to Prasen!" Satrajeet openly accused him.

"What nonsense is this? I asked it for the king, not for myself!" Krishna felt his anger rise at the ridiculous accusation.

"That was only a pretext... you wanted it for yourself!" Satrajeet shouted.

"You shouldn't be accusing anyone unless you are able to prove it." Krishna returned.

"If only I could prove it, you would be in the gallows!" Satrajeet retorted.

"I urge the king to decide on this," Krishna appealed to Ugrasen.

"I cannot decide without proof," King Ugrasen said, "either Chief Satrajeet should produce proof of the crime or Prince Krishna should produce proof of his innocence."

Both Satrajeet and Krishna were dismissed and they went to their homes, angry with each other.

"You are upset, my love," Rukmini remarked, looking at a visibly distraught Krishna when he returned to his palace.

"Indeed, I cannot rest unless and until I have the smear of this accusation removed."

He sent for Balram and Satyaki. They discussed at length the course of action to be taken.

They found out that Prasenjeet normally went to the dense forest at the foot of Mount Raivatak. Next morning Krishna along with a group of Yadav trackers left for the forest. After they had gone for some distance in the forest, the path petered out. Looking for signs of the lost hunter, they crossed streams and densely wooded areas.

"Look here, hoof marks!" a tracker exclaimed, pointing to marks left by a horse on moist ground.

"The horse is loaded, judging from the depth of the mark,"

another of the trackers opined.

Excited, they followed the marks and horse droppings. They led them to a spot on the slope of a hillock. Then they stopped short as they spotted the torn bodies of the horse and the rider. They examined the bodies. They had already started decaying. The rider's chest had been torn and his face badly disfigured.

"It is definitely Prasenjeet," a Yadav remarked, he recognized pieces of his vest.

"It looks like some wild animal got him," Krishna said. "Search him for the jewel."

They searched but did not find Syamantak on him.

"Look at these pug marks," another tracker pointed out. "They seem to be of a big cat, either tiger or lion. Surely a beast has killed them."

They followed the marks into a valley. At the bottom of the valley they found signs of a heavy encounter. Twigs were broken and the grass was flattened.

"Here!" one of the party remarked from behind a clump of trees. They rushed to him to find the mutilated body of a great lion.

"Did the aborigines get it?" Krishna asked.

"No, look at the claw marks," a tracker sitting on his haunches next to the carcass pointed out the lion's head. "And here are spots where the attacker has bitten of chunks of flesh."

"Another lion?" Krishna asked. "Which animal can be so powerful as to kill a lion?"

They looked around and found more pug marks.

"They're definitely a bear's marks," the trackers opined, "and a very large and heavy one at that."

Cautiously with weapons drawn, they followed the marks to the wooded hills. The marks led to a cave.

"The bear must be in there," Krishna said. He looked at the trackers who nodded. "What if we made loud sounds? Will it come out?"

"On the contrary, it might retreat deeper in its safe place," a tracker said.

"Then we shall have to go in," Krishna said

The trackers seemed reluctant to enter the cave.

"I shall go in, I have to find the jewel to prove my

innocence," Krishna remarked. "This is my mission. You stay here."

"Give us a shout if you see it," they said. "Don't try to face it alone."

Krishna girded his loins and entered the cave crouching. It was a tunnel-like entrance much deeper than he had thought. After he had gone some distance the tunnel widened and the roof also rose higher. He could easily stand now. In the light seeping in through the mouth he could see the far walls but no bear. Suddenly he realized there was another tunnel leading at right angles at the very end of the space. He peeped around the cave wall. The space was even wider and there was light coming in from the other end. He ventured into the space. At the end of the space he could see trees and shrubs. When he reached the end he was surprised to see a large space open to the sky but surrounded all around by steep cliffs. There were trees and a pond. He went and stood in the middle of that space. He noticed there were several caves opening on the cliff walls. It was an amazing structure like a deep bowl in the midst of the hills, hidden from the world. The bear had found a wonderful space to live. He was thinking of entering each cave when he heard a voice addressing him.

"Who are you human? And how dare you enter my home?"

He whirled around to see a tall and magnificent bear standing on its hind legs and speaking the human tongue.

"I am Jambuwant, the King of Bears," the bear said with obvious pride. "I led the bear division in Lord Ram's army during the Lanka expedition."

"I am Krishna, a mere cowherd from Gokul," Krishna said with a smile.

"Why have you come here, cowherd?"

"I came in search of a lost jewel." Krishna asked, "Have you seen it?"

"I did obtain a jewel after defeating a lion," Jambuwant replied.

"That must be the one, then," Krishna said. "The lion had killed Prasenjeet of the Yadavs. Prasenjeet had received it from the Sun God. So the jewel belongs to the Yadavs."

"I acquired it after defeating a lion," Jambuwant repeated,

"if you defeat me in a wrestling match you can have it."

"As you wish," Krishna said.

"We will follow all the rules set for such a match," Jambuwant said. "The match will end only when one of us concedes defeat."

They prepared for the bout. Jambuwant chose a clear spot near the pool. They grappled with each other. Although Jambu was taller and stronger, Krishna was agile and skilled. They pulled and pushed and threw each other on the ground. They wrestled the whole day and whole night when the moon shone above the hills illuminating the enclosure. None of them could defeat the other and the match went on for days together.

The Yadav party outside waited for some days and came to the conclusion that Krishna had been killed by the bear. They returned to Dwarika with the news. Balram was enraged when the trackers reported Krishna's demise.

"How can that be possible? You idiots, if he is dead why you didn't bring his body back?" he thundered. "Come on Satyaki, let us go to the spot and find out."

While Balram and the Yadavs were heading for the forest, Jambuwant was exhausted fighting Krishna. Krishna caught him in a hold and threw him on the ground. At last Jambuwant realized this was no ordinary human he was facing.

"You are Vishnu! I accept my defeat," Jambuwant said. "Only Lord Ram and the great ape Hanuman are stronger than me. You must be the Great Lord himself in a new incarnation." Jambuwant bowed to Krishna. "How stupid of me not to recognize you!"

Krishna merely smiled. Jambuwant clapped and his wife watching them quietly from one of the adjoining caves stepped out. "Bring some refreshments for our Lord," he told her.

He made Krishna sit on a large boulder and offered fruits and honey.

"Here is the jewel you seek," he offered the Syamantak. "And I offer you my daughter Jambwvati as your wife."

He asked his wife to fetch Jambuwati. Keen to make friends with different tribes, Krishna accepted her hand. Krishna bade farewell to Jambuwant and started for home with Jambuwati.

As he reached the edge of the forest, he met Balram and

Satyaki coming towards the forest. They were overjoyed to see each other and embraced. They arranged for Prasenjeet's body to be brought to Dwarika for cremation.

"I deeply regret accusing you of the murder of my brother and taking the jewel," Satrajeet said for the umpteenth time when he learnt Krishna had recovered the jewel.

"I had to clear my name," Krishna replied.

There was much joy in Dwarika when Krishna returned unscathed. After Prasenjeet's funeral, King Ugrasen convened a special meeting of the Yadav heads. Krishna handed over Syamantak to Satrajeet in a full court.

"As a token of my repentance, please accept this jewel," Satrajeet said, when Krishna declined, he added, "Then please accept my three daughters Satyabhama, Vratini and Padmavati as you wives."

Krishna went in search of a jewel and found four wives more precious than any jewel in the world. He arranged for separate palaces for Rukmini, Jambuwati, Satyabhama and her two sisters. Satyabhama, in particular, was an exceptional woman. She was trained in martial arts and was outspoken, brave and daring. With Krishna's support she recruited the Yadav women in a fighting force.

One morning their father sent for Krishna and Balram. When they reached there they found Vasudev and Devaki in a melancholic mood.

"Do you remember my sister Kunti?" Vasudev asked.

"We have never met her, but heard a lot from you about her." Balram said. "Wasn't she married to the Kuru King?"

"Yes you remember right. She is no more." Devaki said.

"Oh, what happened?" Krishna asked.

"She along with her five sons had gone to Varnavat for a festival. The mansion she was staying in caught fire and was incinerated. It seems none of them could escape. They were all reduced to ashes."

"This is hard to believe," Krishna pondered over this information. "Usually someone or the other does escape a fire."

"Come on Krishna," Balram said, "you never take any news straight."

"I want you to go to Varnavat," Vasudev said ignoring the

two brothers' banter. "No bodies were found, so there can be no cremation. But their Kuru family is holding funeral rites. You shall represent me there."

That very day Krishna and Balram left for Varnavat. When they arrived there, they went straight to the site of the mishap. The building was totally burned down. They examined the ruins.

"They only found remains of some charred bones in the bedrooms, milord," the officer guarding the site informed them.

"What do you have to say now?" Balram asked Krishna.

"Time will tell," was Krishna's cryptic reply.

After examining the site the two brothers went to the house allotted to them for their stay. They spent a restless night. The rites were to be performed in the morning. However, when they woke up in the morning they were surprised by the arrival of Krishna's wife Satyabhama. She had travelled whole night and seemed very distraught.

"My father has been murdered!" she said as soon as she got down from the coach.

"Who killed Satrajeet? What was the motive? Tell me everything," Krishna asked, after he pacified her. Balram offered her a floral wine which he always carried with him.

"My father went to bed as usual leaving the window open. The thief must have entered through it. The jewel is missing!" Satyabhama replied.

"Then that must be the motive," Krishna said, thinking of who could have done it.

"You must punish the culprit," Satyabhama urged Krishna.

"Yes, we must leave for Dwarika immediately," Krishna told Balram. "Anyway, I did not want to perform the funeral rites for I do not believe that Kunti and her sons are dead. But, please don't mention my hunch to anyone yet, for it seems the Pandavs want to remain hidden, Balram."

When they returned to Dwarika, Krishna went straight to King Ugrasen.

"A thief was seen leaving Satrajeet's mansion," Ugrasen told Krishna. "He has been recognized and I have sent men to arrest him."

Just then the officer sent to apprehend the thief came back.

"He is not to be found in his home, milord," he reported. "Some people have seen him on the road to Mithila."

"I will pursue him," Krishna said. He ordered his chariot to be made ready.

"Sire, the thief was seen riding an excellent horse which is famed for travelling a hundred miles without stopping," the officer informed Krishna.

"In that case I will take two sets of horses for the chariot," Krishna's charioteer replied. "We can rotate them at the yoke so they won't be exhausted."

"I will accompany you," Balram said when the chariot was ready for the chase.

Although they had travelled all the way from Varnavat to Dwarika, Krishna and Balram immediately embarked on the chase to catch the killer.

Daruk, Krishna's expert charioteer drove fast. They stopped only to change the horses.

"There! That must be the horse that could do only a hundred miles." On the road to Mithila, a hundred miles from Dwarika, the charioteer pointed to a dead horse by the roadside.

"Ah, you are right. Driven to the limit it has succumbed," Krishna said. "I think we will soon find the rider, he must be travelling on foot now."

A few miles ahead they spotted a lone traveller running towards the city of Mithila. At the sound of the approaching chariot, the man turned. He recognized Krishna's chariot, left the road and took cover behind a clump of bushes amidst rocks by the road side.

Krishna halted his chariot and started to approach the thief on foot. As a couple of arrows went humming by Krishna quickly ducked behind a tree. The thief got up and started running again. Krishna nocked an arrow, thinking, *"I will shoot him in the leg so he can't run."*

That very moment the thief turned and saw Krishna raise his bow, he crouched to dodge the arrow, but since it was aimed low, it caught him straight in the chest and he collapsed.

Krishna ran to the fallen man. The man was already dead when he reached him. He searched his person and his bag but did not find the jewel.

"He didn't have the jewel on him," Krishna told Balram

when he reached the chariot. "I wanted to catch him alive, but now we have lost the connection. The chase has been futile."

"Are you telling the truth?" Balram flared up all of a sudden. "I don't think so. You want to keep that jewel for yourself! I don't want to come to Dwarika."

He wouldn't listen to Krishna's entreaties. In a huff Balram went away to the city of Mithila. An exasperated Krishna returned alone to Dwarika with the mystery of the jewel unsolved.

Back in Dwarika Krishna waited for news of his aunt Kunti and her sons. He was certain they had escaped the conflagration and sooner or later would reveal themselves. He also kept wondering whom the thief had given the jewel.

One morning Akrur, the minister, invited all the important people to a religious ceremony. He has been spending on religious rites of late. He held grand sacrifices on every full moon.

"I wonder from where he gets the resources to host such a ceremony," Krishna said to his wife Satyabhama. "Hasn't it been said that the person who has the Syamantak jewel becomes wealthy?"

"You have a point there, my dear," Satyabhama replied.

They attended Akrur's ceremony which was conducted in a grand manner. There were feasts and music and chanting of mantras. Almost everybody in Dwarika was present. At the end of the ceremony as Akrur sat contentedly with King Ugrasen, Krishna approached him.

"Tell me, do you or do you not have the Syamantak jewel?" he looked straight in Akrur's eyes.

"I? No..." Akrur fumbled in his reply.

"Don't lie! I want the truth!" Krishna's voice was stern.

"Yes, I admit I have it, the thief had given it to me for safe-keeping," Akrur said in a small voice. He produced the jewel hidden in a box. "You take this jewel, Krishna, you deserve to have it."

"No!" Krishna said. "Give it to King Ugrasen, as head of all Yadav tribes, he deserves to have it."

Krishna sent word to Balram. Pacified he returned to Dwarika now that the jewel had been found.

8. Panchali and the Pandavs

"We have been invited to a groom-choosing ceremony by King Drupad of Panchal," King Ugrasen announced in a meeting of the Yadavs. "His daughter Princess Panchali also known as Draupadi will choose a groom for her from among the assembled braves."

"We must attend the ceremony," Krishna said.

"Are you considering yourself a candidate?" Balram pulled Krishna's leg.

"Oh, come on," Krishna laughed. "I want to attend because I think something important is going to happen there."

"You and your hunches!" Balram said rolling his eyes. Krishna merely smiled at his brother.

They reached Kampilya, the Panchal capital, a day before the appointed day. Kings, princes, savants, adventurers, merchants, bards, traders, mendicants, and tricksters from lands near and far converged on the city of Kampilya, eager to see who the princess would choose for her husband. Footmen ran ahead of chariots to clear a way through the busy streets for their masters. Bullock carts with wheels as tall as a man and loaded with people, food and goods of all sorts creaked on their way to the city.

High arches were erected at all entrances to the city to welcome guests. Water-workers with leather water tanks strapped to their backs sprinkled scented water through hand-held nozzles on the roads to keep the dust down. Music was played from a high tower overlooking the city.

King Drupad provided special quarters for the Yadav brothers within his palace. Princess Draupadi, along with her brother Dhrushtadyumna, went to see Krishna. Krishna sat on the balcony outside his room playing the bamboo flute. The music he played was so sweet that the birds from the garden surrounding the palace had gathered on the trees nearby; deer and rabbits perked up their ears. Draupadi and

Dhrushtadyumna were transfixed by the divine music. It was as if a spell had been cast over the palace. They had heard tales of the entire village of Gokul, where Krishna had grown up amongst cowherds, being enchanted by his flute. At last, when Krishna stopped playing, the trance was broken. Draupadi and Dhrushtadyumna approached and bowed to him. Gifted with endearing manners he became a friend to them. Draupadi developed an instant rapport with him treating him as an elder brother. In no time, Krishna gained her full trust and confidence.

At dawn on the day of the ceremony, people woke up to a long and loud drum roll from the tower of Kampilya. Music played by talented musicians of renown, followed the drums. Soon a steady stream of guests started arriving at the amphitheatre.

A small dais had been erected in the centre of the hall. A glittering metal fish with a hole in place of its eye revolved atop the dais. A large oil bath with a dark bottom was placed in the centre of this dais and reflected the metal fish revolving above.

There were separate rows of seats for different classes of citizens arranged in concentric circles around the contraption of the fish. The royals were at the front, the merchants were behind them whereas the *Brahmins,* the priest class were seated right at the back. When the Yadav brothers entered the hall, King Drupad made Krishna and Balram sit in a prominent place from where they had a good view of the hall.

Famed royal warriors were received by King Drupad. Many eminent sages were present with their favourite pupils. The celestial beings—the *Gandharvs,* the *Siddhs,* and the *Yakshs*—also arrived. They were accompanied by celestial damsels, the *Apsaras* and celestial musicians *Kinnars.* Their arrival filled the venue with heady perfumes. Various deities also came to witness this extraordinary ceremony. Among them were Agni, the deity of fire, Kuber, the treasurer to the gods, and Ashwins, the physicians to gods.

When the guests were all seated, King Drupad sent a message to his son, Prince Dhrushtadyumna, to escort his sister Draupadi. He arrived to the strains of music, with Draupadi following in exquisite silks. A hush fell over the hall as young and old watched the princess of breath-taking beauty. Cream and red silk robes set off her smooth, dark skin. Gold pins adorned her long braided hair. All eyes were riveted to her as the princess of celestial beauty moved down the aisle, setting hearts on fire. After bowing to the king, she occupied a seat set among flowers on a small rostrum near the king's throne.

Krishna was busy watching the assembled people instead of the princess. He scanned the crowd to see if the Pandavs had arrived in some disguise. As Krishna's eyes fell on the priests, he nudged his elder brother, Balram.

"There they are in disguise as *Brahmins*. I am sure the fair person in the group of five in the corner is Kunti's eldest son Yudhisthir. Behind him tall and stout boy is none other than her second son Bheem and the dark-skinned one with supple arms sitting next to him is the third son Arjun. And there near that pillar are the twins, youngest of them all."

"Come on, Krishna," Balram chided his younger brother, "you are so obsessed with the Pandavs, you see them everywhere." Krishna did not reply at that, but smiled to himself.

King Drupad did not recognize the Pandavs, but he kept hoping that somehow Kunti's son, the great archer Arjun would miraculously arrive and claim the princess. There were growing rumours that the Pandavs had escaped the fire at Varnavat. None of the other kings and princes spotted the Pandavs, as their sights were set on Draupadi. The shafts of the deity of love struck the Pandav brothers too. Their eyes were riveted on the maiden adorning the rostrum.

A holy fire was built and mantras recited by the priests of Kampilya. After the rites were over, the chief priest requested King Drupad to commence the main ceremony. The Panchal king turned to his son, Dhrushtadyumna, who bowed to his father and strode to the centre of the hall.

"The kingdom of Panchal is honoured to receive you all, famous warriors and rulers of Aryavart," he began. "We have here a target, a fish revolving over the pan of oil. Any person who desires to win the hand of my sister Draupadi will have to string this bow and shoot five arrows through the eye of the fish looking at its reflection in the oil below. Princess Draupadi will choose the groom from the ones who accomplish this feat."

A murmur spread through the assembled. It presented

a formidable challenge even to those princes well trained in weapons. King Drupad had ordered the creation of this apparatus so that only the greatest of archers could accomplish the task and who, other than Arjun, was the greatest of archers?

Although each of them was eager to win the gorgeous Draupadi, the assembled warriors looked at each other to see who would be the first to take up the challenge. To the amusement of the spectators, several of them stood up at once and sat down again seeing the others rise. At last, Duryodhan, the prince from Hastinapur, cousin to the Pandavs, stepped forward and approached the dais in the centre. He lifted the bow, but was surprised by its weight. Drupad had caused the bow to be made of very strong steel. The prince held the bow in his left hand, with one end resting on the ground, and tried to bend and string it. The bow stayed rigid and did not budge at all. Taking a deep breath and summoning all the strength of his mighty arms, he tried again. The muscles on his arms bulged and it seemed his veins would burst with the effort. The steel bent a little, but was far too straight for the string to be passed. The prince made one last effort, biting his lower lip. He stood stunned, as he realized he had failed. Duryodhan returned to his seat, the swagger gone out of his walk.

The assembled princes realized that this was no simple bow. One after the other, the royals tried and met the same fate. They walked in wearing beautiful crowns, garlands and bracelets and after trying to string that bow, they walked back to their seats panting, with dishevelled crowns and garments. Some who tried to bend the bow by holding it between their knees or feet fell down on their knees. Soon the ardour of those royals was cooled and they gave up hope of possessing the maiden of celestial beauty.

Then, Karn, a friend of Duryodhan, got up. He was a renowned archer, but it was said that he came from a charioteer family. He managed to string the bow, but before he could take up an arrow Draupadi declined to have him as a groom. Crestfallen, he went back to his place.

An uneasy silence pervaded the auditorium as everyone waited for something to happen. The glittering metal fish whirred in the centre. Light streaked through the coloured silks covering the roof and formed patterns on the ground.

A white-clad figure rose quietly from the ranks of the *Brahmins*. All eyes turned to watch the youth Krishna had pointed out to Balram as Arjun. He walked with a steady grace across the marble lined floor towards the centre of the amphitheatre.

"Look at his shoulders and powerful arms," some among the assembled commented. "His confident walk is the sign of a victor."

But some among the royals did not like that a poor *Brahmin* should attempt where the royals had failed. They jeered at him.

Arjun arrived in front of Drupad's throne and joined his hands in Namaste. King Drupad indicated his permission by raising his hand.

Arjun went to the dais and took a close look at the metal fish and its reflection in the oil tub. He appeared to study the convex surface of the oil and noted that it distorted the image and the speed of the fish revolving above. He moved to the stand, lifted the bow and strung it with one smooth movement. Before the gasps of surprised admiration had subsided, he fixed an arrow on the bow and crouched below the target with one knee touching the ground. He fixed his gaze on the reflection in the oil and pausing for a brief moment, shot through the eye of the fish. Unmindful of the pandemonium that broke out in the hall, he sent four more unerring arrows in quick succession through the target.

The *Brahmins* applauded, waving their deerskins and water pots made of coconut shells. Trumpets blared as an eager Draupadi approached Arjun and placed a garland around his neck, signifying her choice. They were now betrothed. The celestials showered flowers on the hero. The musicians struck up in concert. Bards and heralds began to chant in sweet tones the praises of the hero who had struck the mark.

King Drupad was delighted that a great archer had won his daughter. So was Krishna. He saw that the elder Pandav and the twins left the hall quietly. But Arjun and Bheem were surrounded by many warriors who were angry that a *Brahmin* had won the princess in their presence. There was an altercation between them. Krishna saw that the situation was on the verge of taking an ugly turn. Drupad's braves rushed to protect the princess and the young man who had won her.

"Hold it friends," Krishna intervened between the two parties. "This young man has won the princess as per the rules laid down by King Drupad. He has every right to wed her."

Krishna being a prominent leader of the Yadavs, the grumbling warriors withdrew. He pacified and made the two brothers leave with the princess.

Krishna clasped Balram's hand. "That archer can be none other than Arjun. And that fair and tall boy is Bheem. Let's follow them quietly," Krishna whispered to Balram as the duo left with the princess. "We shall be able to meet our aunt." This time, Balram nodded his agreement.

They quietly came out of the hall. They did not take their chariot but followed on foot. They saw Arjun walk with Draupadi while powerful Bheem followed them in a protective manner. They went through the winding streets of Kampilya to the Potter's alley where the Pandavs had found lodging. They saw the trio enter a potter's house. Krishna and Balram reasoned that the eldest brother Yudhisthir and the youngest twins must have already reached home as they had left earlier. They hid around the corner and gave them some time settle down. Then Krishna knocked on the door.

"I am Krishna, Vasudev's son. And this is Balram, my elder brother," Krishna said as the door opened.

"Come in," Yudhisthir admitted them in the house. "Yes, we heard the *Brahmins* mention your names when you were welcomed by the King."

Krishna and Balram bowed to Kunti and she blessed the Yadav brothers. The Pandavs were all delighted to see their cousins of whom they had heard so much but never met.

"Now tell me what happened at Varnavat," Krishna asked after he was offered a seat on a mat.

"Well," Kunti said, "to cut a long story short, you know I was married to the late King Pandu from Hastinapur. My husband and I lived in the hills of the Himalayas for some time. After he passed away, the sons of his brother Dhrutarashtra, who now rules the kingdom, envied my sons. My son, being eldest of all the cousins, was appointed as the crown prince. Duryodhan, whom you must have seen at the ceremony today, had us sent to Varnavat and devised a plan to burn us down. But we escaped through a tunnel. After wandering through the forests, we arrived here."

"I am so happy that you have all escaped the trap at Varnavat and are safe. But we had better leave now or people will discover your identity," Krishna said.

"Let us see what step King Drupad takes next," Kunti said. "Please convey my regards to your parents."

Krishna and Balram took their leave and left the potter's abode. They went back to their quarters in Drupad's palace and awaited the next developments.

Next day they came to know that King Drupad invited the Pandavs to his palace. After a long discussion between them, the King came to know of their identity and was delighted to know they were Pandavs. In a surprising development, all the Pandavs decided to collectively marry the princess.

"This is preposterous!" Balram said when he heard of the decision.

"No, my brother," Krishna explained, "this is a common custom among the natives in the hills of the Himalayas where the Pandavs were brought up."

Amidst great festivities, King Drupad gave away his daughter Draupadi in marriage to the Pandav brothers. All the friends and relatives of the king, ministers of state, and citizens attended the wedding. Some of the kings and princes who had come for the groom-choosing ceremony also were present. In the grand amphitheatre, decked with lotuses and lilies, they all took their seats according to their ranks, wearing ceremonial attire.

On the first day of the five-day ceremony, Yudhisthir married the exotic Panchal princess. The bride and bridegroom wore rich silks, ornaments and marks of sandal paste. They circled the holy fire to the chanting of mantras by priests in the presence of the bride's parents and brother. There were numerous ceremonies performed before the feast and after.

Bheem, Arjun, and the twins, Nakul, and Sahdev celebrated their marriage with the beautiful princess on consecutive days. The Pandavs enjoyed their stay with their common bride in a special palatial building given to them by Drupad.

Guests returned to their respective lands after the five-day wedding ceremony. News of the extraordinary marriage of Draupadi with five husbands travelled all over the land of Aryans with them. Krishna and Balram presented innumerable gifts along with his blessings for the Pandavs and returned to Dwarika.

9. From Rags to Riches

Krishna and Balram arrived in Dwarika from Kampilya towards nightfall. The night watch had already shut the gates to the city at sundown. They were happy and impressed at the vigilance maintained by the Yadavs in their capital.

As Krishna's chariot approached the city gates, the watch recognized him and lowered the drawbridge. Krishna spotted a group of people near the gate. Strangers who arrived in the night would not be admitted to the city, and had to wait there till sunrise, when after identifying their purpose, they could enter the city.

Krishna's eye caught a lean figure sitting alone on a stone bench. The figure appeared familiar. Krishna ordered his charioteer Daruk to stop. He asked the guard to call the person. As the man—a *Brahmin* dressed in a tattered white loin cloth—came closer, Krishna jumped from the chariot in excitement.

"Sudama!" he exclaimed.

The man hesitated for a moment then a smile lit up his weary face. Krishna gave him a big hug.

"What a surprise!" Krishna said, "It has been years since we met. I often think of you and the days we spent as boys in Gokul and the days we spent in Sage Sandipani's ashram."

Before Sudama could speak, Krishna took his hand and led him to his chariot. They both smiled at each other, while Krishna talked excitedly.

"When did you come? I am sorry you had to wait, I was out. I am arriving straight from Draupadi's wedding."

"I have been h...here only for an hour," Sudama could barely speak for the powerful emotions surging through his mind. He held back his tears with an effort.

Krishna noticed that though Sudama seemed happy to meet him, he was ill at ease. His feet were dirty and his clothes dusty. He had wanted to take his childhood friend to his quarters, but he realized it might make him more uncomfortable, so Krishna asked his attendant to take Sudama to the guest rooms.

"You look tired and so am I from the journey. Let us meet for supper in an hour," he pressed Sudama's hand and went to his palace.

Sudama's mind was a whirlwind of emotions. He had travelled on foot for days to reach Dwarika. Actually he had been quite reluctant to come to Dwarika, but his wife had pestered him. He could not blame her either. There was hardly anything to feed the children. Sudama had not fared too well after completion of his education. His parents had died soon after his marriage. He and his wife had somehow managed on the meagre alms and gifts which he received for the services he rendered as a priest. But after their children were born, the situation became desperate. Learning of the prosperous Dwarika, his wife wanted him to go to Krishna for help. Sudama desisted for a long time, as he did not believe in taking advantage of his childhood friend. At last he gave in for the sake of his children.

While leaving for Dwarika, he thought of taking a gift for his friend, but there was nothing in the house. His wife found a handful of beaten rice at the bottom of a vessel and Sudama tied it in a small cloth and left for Dwarika

In the luxurious guest house in Dwarika Sudama took a bath; the cool water was refreshing and he felt better. He found fresh white cotton clothes laid out for him. He thought of his children as he donned the clothes–the poor things had never worn new clothes, always old clothes given away by people.

There was a gentle knock on the door and Krishna entered. Sudama tried to hide the bundle containing the flattened rice, but Krishna noticed it.

"Ah," he said, "sister-in-law must have sent some gift for me. Come on, give it to me."

Sudama felt embarrassed. The knot of old cloth seemed so out of place in that palace. He gingerly proffered it. Krishna took it, sat cross-legged on a settee and opened it with eagerness.

"Wow," he exclaimed, "beaten rice! You haven't forgotten how I love it, then." He chewed with great relish. Servants from the palace kitchen arrived with gold plates and pots and set the meal for them. Thinking of his hungry little ones back at home Sudama could hardly bring himself to eat the delicacies they served, but Krishna pressed him offering many dishes.

After supper Krishna led him to the balcony overlooking the garden. They sat in the cool breeze flowing in from the sea. They indulged in their reminiscences about their time as students. Krishna told him about his exploits–the defeat of Kans, setting up of Dwarika, meeting with the Pandavs.

As they spoke, Sudama's woes were forgotten. He let Krishna talk. The very presence of Krishna by his side made him feel so peaceful. He experienced spiritual ecstasy the like of which he had only glimpsed in deep meditation occasionally. It was late in the night when they parted for the night. Sudama, tired by the journey, slept a sound sleep that night in the rest house.

When he got up the next morning, the sweet music of Krishna's flute filtered through his window. After a while the music stopped and Krishna himself arrived to show him the city of Dwarika, the Raivatak mountains and the sea shore. They spent several days visiting places.

At last one morning, Sudama told Krishna, "I must... leave now, my wife and ch...children must be waiting for my return."

"Oh yes, I understand. My charioteer Daruk will drive you home, Sudama," Krishna told him.

He bid farewell to Krishna and left for his village, feeling peaceful and content. Halfway through, he realized that he had not asked Krishna for anything to alleviate his poverty. On the one hand he did not regret it; he had not let their friendship be tainted. On the other, his financial worries continued. He had failed to fulfil his family's expectations.

Charioteer Daruk dropped him off at the outskirts of the village. Sudama thanked him and entered his village towards evening, a forlorn dejected figure walking with his head hung low. As he turned the corner of the street he lived on, his heart lurched wildly. His house was not to be seen. There was a building, but it looked different. A woman in rich silks was lighting lamps. Children clad in nice dresses were playing with colourful toys.

"*Taat, taat,*" the children shouted as they rushed to him. Then he realized they were his children. And the woman was no stranger, she was his wife.

He picked up the youngest child and another held his finger, yet another clung to his leg.

"We have been waiting for you," his wife smiled at him.

"But, w...whatever happened to our house? Where did you get all these... clothes?" he asked bewildered.

"Oh, don't you know?" she replied, "the day after you went to Dwarika, Krishna sent his people. They brought these clothes and toys and sacks full of rice and grains and a chest full of gold coins and repaired our house and painted it and built a stable and put cows and heifers there. What is more he has conferred an annuity upon you!" She said all in one breath, her face flushed with excitement. He stood gaping at her.

That night, Krishna met him in his dream.

"Why did you send all this, Krishna?" Sudama asked.

"I accepted and enjoyed your gift, didn't I? You should accept mine gracefully."

"I offered only a handful of parched rice, Krishna."

"You gave me all that you had, Sudama. I have given a mere fraction of what I have. Your gift to me is a million times more valuable than what I gave you."

Sudama had no answer to that one.

"The blind Kuru King Dhrutarashtra has received the Pandavs well at Hastinapur," King Ugrasen informed the assembly of Yadavs. "He has also divided the kingdom between Duryodhan and Pandavs and conferred upon them the old capital of Khandavprasth."

"That is great news!" Krishna remarked. "I must meet the Pandavs and help in setting up the new capital."

"Me too," Balram joined him. He left for Hastinapur that very day.

After arriving at Hastinapur they first met Bhishm, the grandsire of the Pandavs. Bhishm was uncle to King Dhrutarashtra and the late King Pandu. The octogenarian was a famed warrior and going strong even at the advanced age.

"Oh Krishna, I am so lucky to have met you," Bhishm said as he offered a seat to Krishna. "I am happy that you are a friend of the Pandavs. They have suffered much in the past and I am sure they will do well with you to guide them."

Next they met the blind ruler of Hastinapur King

Dhrutarashtra and his brother Vidur, the renowned minister of the Kurus.

At last they went to meet the Pandavs and aunt Kunti in their quarters. The Pandavs were delighted to see Krishna.

"Our fortunes have turned since we met you, Krishna," Yudhisthir, the eldest Pandav welcomed him. "We are so happy you have joined us when we have been granted a land of our own and all set to develop a new kingdom."

"So our beloved uncle has now bestowed those ruins on us!" Bheem, the middle Pandav, made a face. He was a powerful wrestler and had a straightforward approach to matters somewhat like Balram.

"Bheem, it does not behove us to show disrespect to elders," Yudhisthir chided him gently.

"Excuse me for saying so, but I think Bheem is right, of what use is that forsaken land to us?" Arjun, the archer, was indignant too.

"I have the answer to that question, my friend," Krishna said. They all turned to him. "That land presents an opportunity to prove your capability. What would the mighty Bheem, skilled Arjun and righteous Yudhisthir do with the well-established kingdom of Hastinapur? Khandav is an opportunity to prove that your claim to the kingdom is not because you are born in the line of the Kurus, but because you deserve it."

Krishna's words lifted the spirits of the Pandavs. They could hardly wait for the proposed coronation ceremony to be over. They started making plans for rejuvenating Khandavprasth.

Dhrutarashtra, in an attempt to gloss over the incident at Varnavat, partly out of genuine affection and partly to make a show of affection for his nephews, arranged a grand ceremony for the coronation of Yudhisthir as King of Khandavprasth. Invitations were sent to all kingdoms and sages of renown. In the presence of a large assembly in the exquisite decorated royal hall at Hastinapur, Dhrutarashtra placed the crown on Yudhisthir's head after the religious rites were performed. After the ceremony, the Pandavs left for Khandav with Kunti, Draupadi, Krishna and Balram.

The ruins of the old city of Khandavprasth were situated in a vast area of thorny brush country stretching for miles. To the west were hills which extended to the South and formed a backdrop to the wilderness. The only respite offered to the beholder were the cool and dark waters of the Yamuna flowing on the eastern edge of the land. After a day's journey in the sun when the caravan of chariots arrived at Khandav, the Pandavs found the sight quite depressing. They got down from the carriages tired and weary. Only Krishna was his normal relaxed self. There was a spring in his step as he jumped down from the chariot and went to the encampment set up by the advance party. The Pandavs followed and dumped their gear.

Krishna had arranged for builders from Dwarika. After Varnavat, they could no longer trust builders from Hastinapur. Krishna summoned the architects. Krishna's enthusiasm was infectious and soon the five brothers got over their depression and were engrossed in planning their capital. They measured out the land to build the city.

Bheem and Balram led a team to clear the debris and overgrowth. Krishna and Arjun led another team to the low hills in the west. They had seen greenery on the hills and concluded there was water underneath. Dark fissures on the face of the hills meant that water streams had once run down the slopes. They spent hours scouting. Towards evening, Krishna pointed out a spot where rocks had tumbled down sometime in the past and blocked the stream. Arjun shot a long arrow between two huge rocks and a jet of water spurted out. A team wielding crowbars moved the rocks and to shouts of jubilation, a stream flowed down the slopes. Within a few days the old moat surrounding the ruins of the city was filled with water. The site was cleared of debris and construction commenced in earnest.

A magnificent city rose from the ruins, looking resplendent like the capital of the celestial kingdom. It stood adorned with palatial mansions and numerous gates, each furnished with a couple of panels resembling the out-stretched wings of Garuda. The missiles of foes would not make the slightest impression on them. It was protected with gateways set in the formidable ramparts which were well-furnished with weapons of attack, darts and other missiles which looked like double-tongued snakes. The walls were lined with numerous warriors along their whole length, and there were thousands of sharp hooks and machines capable of slaying hundreds of enemy warriors. Other machines with large iron wheels designed to spit fire were planted on the battlements.

The wide, well laid out streets within were lined with shady trees; traffic flowed easily and there was no chance of congestion or accident. The city, decked with innumerable mansions, came to be known as Indraprasth as it was like the celestial capital of Indra, the king of gods. In the centre of the city rose the palace of the Pandavs. Built in marble and filled with rare novelties, it drew crowds of visitors.

When the city was built, the prospects of earning wealth drew numerous merchants from lands far and near and they set up businesses. Renowned artists arrived, wishing to take up their abode there. A thriving economy soon emerged. Several learned men and women, well-acquainted with all the scriptures and conversant with many languages, knowing that their knowledge would be appreciated and valued, came and settled at Indraprasth.

Around the city were laid out many delightful gardens adorned with rare trees. Citizens spent their leisure hours in the shade of branches bent down with the weight of blossoming fragrant flowers and fruit. The gardens came alive with feathery creatures of various kinds and the verdant groves always resounded with the notes of peacocks and blackbirds.

There were various houses within those parks for relaxation and numerous bowers of creepers. Charming artificial hillocks were surrounded by lakes of crystal water and delightful tanks, fragrant with lotuses and lilies, populated with swans and ducks and singing birds.

The Pandavs felt grateful to Bhishm for advising Dhrutarashtra to bestow that land on them, and to Krishna for his guidance. Yudhisthir ruled the large kingdom peopled with creative, industrious, brave and pious men and women.

When the construction of Indraprasth came to a close, Krishna and Balram decided to leave. Balram announced that he was going to Hastinapur to impart lessons in mace to Duryodhan as he had been doing for Bheem while at Indraprasth.

Krishna decided to return to Dwarika. The Pandavs bid him farewell with a heavy heart. Draupadi and Arjun had become quite attached to Krishna and felt very sad.

"You must visit Dwarika," Krishna told them.

"How I would love to," Arjun said, "but this new kingdom is going to demand all our attention in the near future. I don't know when I will be able to see Dwarika."

Little did Arjun know that he would soon be leaving Indraprasth and eventually visit Dwarika.

10. A Sister's Solace

Krishna was having lunch with his wife Satyabhama in her mansion. She had appointed a new chef from Mithila and they were enjoying the delicacies.

"Arjun has been expelled from Indraprasth," Krishna said tasting the exquisite wine from Mithila.

"Oh, why?" Satyabhama was surprised.

"You know the Pandavs have Draupadi as their common wife. Now Sage Narad, when he visited them, asked them to make a rule about their relation with her so that there would be no dispute."

"Yes, I have heard about it. They stipulated that if one of them was enjoying her company none other would disturb them."

"That's right. It so happened that Arjun had forgotten his bow in Draupadi's palace and Yudhisthir was with her when he went to retrieve it. So according to the terms of their rule, he has to stay away from Indraprasth for twelve years."

"That is so sad," Satyabhama said, "where did the poor man go?" she asked as she signalled the maid to refill Krishna's chalice.

"Well, as it turns out he isn't such a poor guy. He first went to the north and married Ulupi the princess of the serpents. Then he went to the east and wedded the mountain king's daughter Chitrangada. Then he went to the south and rescued five Apsaras trapped in lakes. I have a feeling he will now come to the west and visit Dwarika."

Another of Satyabhama's maid entered the dining room and bowed to Satyabhama, "King Ugrasen has sent a messenger to report to the Lord, milady."

"Show him in," Satyabhama said.

"Arjun, the Pandav prince has arrived on the west coast, sire," a Yadav guard coming in from the coast informed Krishna.

"Oh good," Krishna said, "I was waiting for this news."

As soon as he finished his meal, Krishna set out for the coast near Dwarika. From a vantage point he saw a solitary figure clad in white tread the sands. Krishna recognized Arjun and got down from the chariot. The two friends met at the edge of the ocean as the sun was setting.

"Ages ago we first met on the banks of the ocean of milk," Krishna said, "you don't remember, but I do. You were Nara and I was Narayan many lives ago. You will gradually remember our previous lives."

They mounted the chariot and Krishna took Arjun to the Raivatak Mountain where preparations for the forthcoming Yadav festival were afoot. The mountain had been adorned by many artificers and stocked with many delicacies. Krishna sat with Arjun and they enjoyed the rehearsals of the actors and the dancers until late in the night. After the humidity of the coastal climate, they found the cool mountain air exhilarating.

Krishna led him to his hill resort. Tired after the long journey, Arjun plonked himself on a bed. As he lay on that soft bed, he told Krishna about the sacred waters, the lakes and the mountains, the rivers and the forests he had seen and the kings and princesses he had met. While he was speaking of these, sleep stole upon him.

Krishna woke up in the morning before Arjun. He started playing his flute. Soon Arjun awoke and they set out for Dwarika. The Yadavs had adorned the city of Dwarika to receive Arjun, first cousin to Krishna. The citizens of Dwarika, eager to see the famed warrior, poured into the streets by thousands. All the leaders of the Bhoj, the Vrishni, and the Andhak clans belonging to the Yadav community had gathered in the main square. Arjun was accorded a tumultuous welcome by them. He, in his turn, bowed to those who deserved his respect, receiving their blessings. The famous hero was received by the young men of the Yadav tribe. Wending through the streets of Dwarika, they went to the delightful mansion of Krishna.

One morning Krishna woke up and found Arjun was not in the guest house.

"He has gone to the garden, milord," a maid informed him. He went to the palace garden and found Arjun talking to his sister Subhadra. Krishna loitered across the grass from the palace corridor.

"So you have met each other already?"

"He hasn't even told me his name." Subhadra said looking at Arjun.

"Let me introduce you," Krishna said, "this is Subhadra, my dear sister and this is Arjun…"

Arjun offered *namaste* with a smile.

Soon Arjun left with Krishna for the Raivatak Mountain where the grand festival of the Yadavs was to begin. The citizens of Dwarika, some on foot and some in chariots, with their wives and followers, arrived there by thousands. There came Ugrasen, the powerful king of the Vrishni race, accompanied by his wives. And there was Lord Balram, roving at will, hilarious with drink, accompanied by his wife Revati. Also present there were Satyaki, Krutavarma, and Akrur—statesmen and heroes of the Yadavs. They roamed there, excited with drink and adorned with floral wreaths of great beauty and with expensive attires, and disported themselves like celestials. When that delightful festival of immense grandeur commenced, musicians struck up in concert and dancers began to dance and the vocalists to sing.

Krishna and Arjun went about together, enjoying themselves. While wandering, they saw Subhadra looking breathtakingly beautiful, decked with ornaments and laughing in the midst of her friends. As soon as Arjun saw her, he was moonstruck. Krishna observed Arjun contemplate her with absorbed attention.

"Can the heart of one who ranges the woods be agitated by the god of desire? Tell me if your heart is fixed upon her. Subhadra is the favourite daughter of my father and he's planning her groom choosing ceremony-*swayamvar*," Krishna said, "But there are complications. Yesterday Balram arrived with a message from Duryodhan that he seeks her hand in marriage. Balram is a wonderful person, but very adamant. No one can say what will happen at the *swayamvar*."

Arjun was alarmed. He looked at Krishna with apprehension. Both fell silent for a few moments.

"I have a feeling she likes you, Arjun. And a true warrior never gives up." Krishna smiled, "She will visit the shrine on the mountain early tomorrow morning."

"Your wish is my command, I will take her away."

"No, Arjun," Krishna said, "I command nothing. You have to make your own decision and be responsible for the actions. I am only offering help. My chariot is available for you if you want to meet her near the shrine. If she likes you, she will go with you to Indraprasth. We'll see what happens next."

That evening, Krishna visited Subhadra. They chatted about the festival for some time.

"I hear you will be marrying Duryodhan," he said all of a sudden.

"What?!" Subhadra was taken aback.

"Balram has brought the proposal from Hastinapur, didn't you know?"

"Duryodhan? Never! That coward tried to burn the Pandavs at Varnavat." Subhadra flared up. "I will never marry him."

"By the way, aren't you going to the Raivatak shrine in the morning?"

"I am? I have no such plan." Subhadra wondered why Krishna had changed the topic.

"Arjun is leaving for Indraprasth early tomorrow," Krishna said, "he will visit the shrine before leaving."

He left her without further elaboration, but she knew what he meant.

The magnificent steeds harnessed to Krishna's chariot stood pawing the ground, their breath forming clouds of vapour in the cold mountain air. Krishna drew Arjun aside.

"Taking Subhadra with you is not the difficult part, my friend," he said, "but her acceptance by Draupadi will be. Remember, Draupadi is born from fire."

Arjun looked worried. Krishna patted his shoulder.

"But it won't be difficult if you remember that Draupadi is also like a sister unto me. Go now and may success be upon you." Arjun turned to leave and as he put a foot on the chariot step, Krishna raised his hand.

"One last thing," Krishna said, "Let Subhadra drive the chariot." Puzzled, Arjun looked at him.

"...For this is her journey more than yours," Krishna completed his sentence.

"As you wish," Arjun said, though he did not understand what Krishna had in mind.

He shook the reins and the eager horses broke into a trot. He drove the chariot towards the shrine atop Raivatak Mountain.

Subhadra's guards and maids rushed back screaming to the royal court at Dwarika, causing a furore.

"Arjun has abducted Subhadra!"

The chief officer of the court, after hearing about the incident from the guards, blew his gold-decked trumpet of loud blare, calling all to arms. Stirred up by that sound, the Yadav braves gathered at once, leaving their meals half eaten. Unable to brook what Arjun had done, a belligerent mood prevailed in the meeting dominated by a furious Balram clad in blue robes and under influence of the flower-wine he was so fond of.

"Arjun has abused our hospitality!" he roared.

"We will catch him and punish him," Satyaki, commander of the Yadav forces declared, tightening the sword belt around his waist.

"Get the chariots ready for pursuit," Krutavarma ordered.

Balram noticed that Krishna sat observing the commotion with a detached calm.

"Why aren't you saying anything?" Balram accosted him. "It was for your sake that we welcomed the ungrateful Pandav. He has stolen your chariot and our sister. It seems that vile wretch did not deserve the honour after all. I shall make the earth destitute of the Pandavs. Never shall I put up with this transgression."

"Hear, hear!" The Yadav warriors stamped their feet roaring their approval of Balram's words.

"In my opinion," Krishna began and the assembly felt silent, "Arjun has not abducted Subhadra." There were groans of protest at that.

"Listen to this," Krishna turned to Subhadra's attendants. "Did Subhadra call out for help?"

"No, sire," came the meek reply.

"Tell us who was driving the chariot when it left for Indraprasth?"

"It was the Princess Subhadra, sire," they said.

"Does this not mean that it was Subhadra who abducted Arjun?" Krishna turned to the Yadav chiefs and they had no answer. "Or, it could be that Subhadra did not want to marry Duryodhan and so she appealed to Arjun to rescue her? And, my dear brother, Arjun has borrowed my chariot, not stolen it. In my opinion Arjun has enhanced the honour of the Yadavs. This alliance is very proper. Subhadra is a renowned maiden and Arjun a great warrior. If they have decided to unite by mutual approval, it is only fair.

"Further," he addressed the generals, "your desire to capture Arjun is unattainable. I do not see any one in the three worlds, except Lord Shiva, who could vanquish him in battle. If Arjun goes to his city after defeating us, the Yadavs will lose face forever. There is no disgrace, however, in conciliation. My advice is to go and bring him back to Dwarika with due respect and let the couple be married in befitting style."

When Krishna finished speaking, the Yadavs were mollified; swords were pushed back in scabbards and the assembly relaxed.

"I knew if Krishna got an opportunity to talk, he would silence us all." Balram threw down his weapon in mock disgust. "Let's send messengers to Arjun now and bring him back with honour."

Riders on swift horses were dispatched to meet Arjun and Subhadra and the couple was happy to return to Dwarika. Vasudev gave away his daughter to Arjun in a grand wedding ceremony. Yudhisthir sent his blessings from Indraprasth.

Arjun stayed the last of his twelve years of exile in Dwarika, spending time with his bride in a special palace in the amazing city and at delightful places on the West Coast. Towards the end of the period of twelve years, Arjun returned to Indraprasth with Subhadra.

Krishna, along with his wife Satyabhama, Balram, Satyaki, Krutavarma, Akrur and other prominent Yadavs arrived at Indraprasth with presents for Arjun, Subhadra and the groom's family. Krishna presented them with chests of gold filled with precious stones. The elder brother Balram, presented a hundred war elephants, decked with coverlets and bells, well-adorned with many ornaments and equipped with majestic thrones on their backs. The Yadavs stayed at Indraprasth, enjoying the beauty and luxury of the splendid city before returning to Dwarika.

Krishna stayed on at Indraprasth after Balram and other Yadav chiefs had left. Along with Arjun he roamed the woods on the banks of Yamuna hunting wild boar and deer. He and Krishna spent the whole morning hunting. When the summer sun reached its zenith, they went for a long swim in the river and were ready for lunch.

"I am tired to the bone," Arjun said as he got out of the waters of Yamuna. They joined Subhadra, Draupadi and Krishna's wife Satyabhama relaxing in the cottages on the banks of the river. After tasting exhilarating wines and indulging in venison, the duo left the royal ladies for a long siesta in the delightful woods.

They lay on the soft grass with a gentle breeze blowing through the trees. As they were drifting to sleep a figure approached them. The man's appearance was so striking they sat bolt upright, sleep forgotten. His complexion was that of molten gold, his eyes were red and clothes yellow exuding the exuberance of the glowing sun.

"I am hungry and ill, will you feed me?" He asked.

"Why, yes..." Arjun said. "Go to the palace kitchen, no one is ever sent away hungry from there."

"The kitchen doesn't have what I need. Only you both have the power to satiate my hunger," the stranger said. "I am no beggar. I am Agni, the god of fire. For many years I have been fed with clarified butter in sacrifices and that has made me weak. I am suffering from surfeit which I cannot dispel. I need to consume this Khandav forest to rejuvenate myself. But every time I try to consume it, Indra the rain god intervenes because his friend the great snake Takshak lives here. Only you possess the weapons to disperse the rain clouds while I consume the forest. Will you help me?"

"Indeed, we will," Krishna said. The Pandavs needed land for cultivation and for habitation. The Khandav forest was overgrown with thorny trees and housed dangerous animals. Over the years the animals had grown so bold they attacked people in broad daylight. Several times hyenas and wolves entered cottages while people were at work and snatched away babies. Tigers and lions took away cattle from stables. Robbers used the forsaken forest as a hideout. The Pandavs had been thinking of ways to reclaim the brush land and this was an opportunity.

"I possess the mighty wind weapon to dispel the clouds, Agni," Arjun said, "but I don't have a suitable powerful bow to launch it."

Agni summoned Varun, the sea god, who produced a magnificent bow called the *Gandiv* and bestowed it on Arjun. This Gandiv bow had been crafted by Brahma, the grandfather of all gods. It was king among all the weapons and the grinder of them all. The Gandiv was faultless in every respect. It was adorned with various colours and very pleasant to look at. Agni also gave two inexhaustible quivers of arrows and a chariot bearing celestial weapons to Arjun. On the flag of that chariot was mounted a large ape with a ferocious face like that of a lion. The chariot was created in person by the architect of the universe. Yoked to that chariot were steeds white as silver of the fleecy clouds and born in the region of Gandharvs.

Varun presented an extraordinary discus to Krishna. "This has been your weapon in previous ages," he said, "I have but kept it for you."

Named Sudarshan Chakra, the disc was razor sharp at the edge and had a thousand spokes. Attached to a hole in the centre of the disc was a handle to wield and throw the disc. It was a fiery weapon capable of vanquishing in battle all foes, even those who were not human and the disc returned to the thrower's hand after accomplishing its task.

Arjun thanked Agni. He circled the chariot and mounted it. He forcibly strung the bow and those who heard the sound it produced quaked with fear. Krishna and Arjun, armed with these celestial weapons, felt confident of countering the thunderbolt of Indra.

Agni went to the edge of the forest and flames blazed forth from his fingers. The robbers hiding in the Khandav forest hurled stones from catapults, but their missiles were shattered in mid-air by Arjun's arrows. The attackers soon realized that they could not match Krishna and Arjun in battle and left that land forever. Arjun and Krishna patrolled the land abutting

Indraprasth, preventing wild beasts from entering it. Pursued by flames, most of the living creatures, uttering frightful yells escaped from the far edge of Khandav forest over the hills and into the dense forests beyond. Some who dwelt in burrows dug deep into the earth and remained safe. Birds flew away and reptiles slithered into crevices and went to the netherworld beyond reach of the fire.

Old, wasted, and dying animals bearing festering wounds infested with maggots could not escape and were caught by Agni and consumed with a flash, relieving them of a long-drawn painful death. While the rest of the birds flew away, a single bird kept circling a tree. Its wingless young were in the nest and the bird could not leave them. It prayed to Agni to spare their lives. Agni acquiesced and did not touch the area where the four young nestlings lived.

Agni started engulfing thorny trees and shrubs and weeds alike. As he burnt fiercely, its seven flames rose high in the sky and the blazing forest looked like a mountain of fire. Mighty flames of the blazing fire reached the firmament and caused great anxiety to the celestials. All the illustrious dwellers in heaven went in a body to their chief, Indra.

"Why does Agni burn that forest below?" they asked, "has the time come for the destruction of the world?"

Hearing these words of the gods and himself having witnessed what Agni was doing, Indra set out for the protection of Khandav. He soon covered the sky with masses of thick black clouds and began to pour rain upon the forest in dense showers. But the showers were all dried up in the sky itself by the heat of the fire and they could not reach the fire at all. Indra, angry with Agni, collected even more huge masses of clouds and caused them to yield heavier downpour. With the flames contending with those heavy showers, and with masses of clouds overhead, the forest filled with smoke and flashes of lightning became terrible to behold. Arjun, invoking his excellent weapons, soon covered the forest with innumerable arrows like a thick fog preventing that shower of rain by Indra.

On the command of Indra, the winds agitated all the oceans with a frightening roar and masses of clouds charged with torrents of rain gathered in the sky. Those elephantine clouds began to pour thick showers and emitted terrible flashes of lightning charged with thunderclaps. Arjun hurled the great weapon *Vayava* after proper mantras to dispel those clouds. With that weapon, Indra's thunderbolt and those clouds were destroyed. The torrents of rain with which those clouds were charged were all dried up and the lightning that played amongst them died down. Within a moment the sky was cleared of dust and darkness, and a pleasant, cool breeze began to blow and the disc of the sun resumed its normal state.

Undeterred, Agni, blazing forth with all his flames and filling the universe with his roars, continued devouring the creatures and vegetation there with glee. The lord of the celestials, riding on his white elephant called Airawat, rushed at those two warriors. Taking up his thunderbolt which was renowned to never go in vain, he hurled it with great force.

"Consider these two humans slain!" he shouted in the grip of excitement. Beholding the fierce thunderbolt about to be hurled by their chief, other celestials also took up their respective weapons. Yam, the god of death, sitting on his buffalo bull took up the death-dealing mace; Kuber the celestial treasurer took up his spiked club. Varun took his noose and Skand the god of war sitting astride his peacock mount raised his long lance. Others took up bows, clubs, darts, battle-axes, and bludgeons bearing sharp spikes, discs and scimitars. The celestials, resplendent with their own energy, rushed against Krishna and Arjun to smite them down. In that great conflict were wonderful portents, resembling those that appeared at the time of the universal dissolution, stunning all the creatures. But Arjun and Krishna, fearless and invincible in battle, calmly waited, bow and disc ready. They assailed the advancing host of celestials with their own thunderous arrows. The celestials, with their weapons shattered by Krishna and Arjun, at last left the field of battle. No one among the celestials mustered there could vanquish Krishna and Arjun in battle. When the celestials saw that they could not protect that forest, they retired from the scene. Indra, seeing the immortals retreat, applauded Krishna and Arjun.

Krishna saw a demon escaping from the home of the serpent King Takshak. Agni, roaring like the clouds pursued him. Krishna stood with his chakra weapon upraised ready to strike him down. On seeing Krishna's discus uplifted and

Agni pursuing from behind to burn him, the demon appealed to Arjun to protect him. Hearing his voice quaking with fear, Arjun rushed to him on his chariot and requested Krishna and Agni to spare him.

The demon was Maya, architect to the demonic world. He told them that the viper Takshak had escaped, because he had left Khandav forest before Agni set it on fire. Takshak's son had also managed to escape, he informed them.

Protected from Indra by Krishna and Arjun, Agni burned that forest for fifteen days and was restored to health. He thanked Krishna and Arjun profusely and left. Six of the forest's dwellers had been saved—Maya the demon, the four young birds who could not fly, and Takshak's serpent son.

Maya sat with Krishna and Arjun on the banks of Yamuna.

"What can I do to repay you for saving my life?" he asked Arjun.

"Don't consider yourself under any obligation, Maya," Arjun said. "Protecting one who seeks asylum is the duty of a *Kshatriya*."

"You are a noble warrior and don't expect any favour in return, but I will build an exquisite palace for you, the like of which has never been seen on earth," the renowned architect offered.

Arjun and Krishna returned to the palace with Maya. Yudhisthir was pleased to learn of Maya's offer to construct a palace. "Build us a palace which will be rare in its combination of the best of demonic, godly and human architecture," he said. "Choose suitable land and we shall lend you all the assistance you desire."

With Indra defeated, rains subsided. Evenings became pleasant.

"Sugarcane has arrived from the farms," Yudhisthir informed Krishna as they sat with Subhadra, Satyabhama, Draupadi and Arjun on the terrace of the palace one evening as the full moon was rising in the east.

"Oh, how I love sugarcane," Subhadra clapped in delight.

"Me too," Satyabhama joined her.

Yudhisthir ordered the servants to bring in the fresh sugarcane.

"Let me chop off the leaves and roots for you, my sister," Krishna said lovingly to Subhadra. He took a machete and started chopping of the ends of the stalks. Suddenly his hand slipped and he nicked his wrist holding the sugarcane.

"Careful, Krishna," Arjun said.

The cut started bleeding profusely.

"Go get some bandage," Subhadra ordered her maid.

"Why wait for the maid," Satyabhama impatient as always, dashed off to get the bandage.

Draupadi rushed forward and without a word simply tore off the end of her expensive sari and bandaged Krishna's wrist before the bandage arrived.

Krishna smiled and thanked his deemed sister Draupadi, realizing she loved him more than his own sister Subhadra. 'I shall not forget her unselfish love,' Krishna said to himself.

The story of Draupadi's great love for Krishna spread in Indraprasth and then in all the kingdoms. To commemorate the sisterly love, people established a custom on the full moon of the last month of monsoons. On this day brothers visit their sisters who tie a colourful band on their wrists.

After a short stay at Indraprasth, Krishna returned to Dwarika with Satyabhama.

11. Of Wives and Vines

Back in Dwarika Krishna lay cuddled with his wife Rukmini in her mansion on a couch decorated with fresh flowers. Rukmini's mansion was next to Satyabhama's, beyond that were the mansions of Jambuwati and the other wives. All those mansions were within Krishna's palace complex and their courtyards were separated by neatly trimmed hedges.

"So, your cousin Arjun has four wives now! Why do you men have to marry so many?" She was referring to the fact that various kings had offered their daughters to Krishna and he had a total of eight wives.

"Well, the reason is simple, my dear," Krishna couldn't but smile at her question. "It is to build political alliances that many marriages among the royals take place."

"It's only an excuse!" she said. "Is that the only reason you married Satyabhama, Jambuwati and the others?"

"Of course," Krishna replied smiling, "you are the only one I married for love."

"Liar!" her soft laughter was like the tinkling of silver bells. "But let me tell you I am not jealous of your other wives. For me it is enough that you love me." She inhaled his hair, scented by a bath with water fragrant with flower petals. "Your hair smells of jasmine."

"And you exude the scent of the blue lotus, my dear," Krishna whispered as he held Rukmini close.

"Speaking of flowers reminds me," Rukmini said, "I hear there is a beautiful tree in Svarg which produces lovely flowers which bloom at night."

"Yes it is called *Parijat*, my dear. It has soft white petals and an orange stem."

"If you visit Svarg any time for some purpose," Rukmini said kissing his ear, "will you bring those flowers for me?"

"Why, of course!" Krishna kissed her back.

"Promise?"

"Promise!" Krishna dearly loved Rukmini for she was as soft-natured as her speech.

Just then they heard a booming sound outside the palace. A pleasant breeze began to blow carrying celestial fragrance and there was a downpour of flowers. Yakshs, the celestial musicians, began to play. Krishna along with the Yadavs rushed out to see what was happening. A great noise, covered with a net of lustre, was heard in the sky. Within that effulgence, the Yadavs saw Indra, seated on Airawat, the white elephant and encircled by deities. Indra's mount landed in the central square of Dwarika. Krishna and King Ugrasen welcomed the king of gods. Alighting from Airawat, the chief of gods embraced Krishna. He bowed to the Yadavs in order of age and rank. Invited by King Ugrasen he entered into the magnificent assembly-hall of Dwarika. King Ugrasen offered him a special seat and proffered various delicacies and wines.

"I have come to meet you today for a specific purpose. You must have heard of this demon King Narakasur from Pragjothishyapur in the east," Indra began. "He is the son of Bhumi, the goddess of earth. He has obtained a boon from the grandsire of gods and become too powerful for his own good. Narakasur has become the leader of the demons, the Asurs. He has assembled all the different tribes of Asurs under his fold. Under his advice they have turned offensive. They are obstructing the paths of the gods. Their armies are invading various regions and plundering all the wealth. They have amassed heaps of gold and jewels in Naraka's capital Pragjothishyapur.

"Naraka isn't satisfied conquering neighbouring kings. He has taken away their queens. He has abducted and abused sixteen thousand and one hundred wives and daughters of humans, the Apsaras and Gandharvs and abused them. He has violated the teenage daughter of god Tvashta. He has imprisoned all these women on mount Mani where he has built a great fortress in the region of the demon Mura.

"And yesterday he has attacked Aditi, the mother of all gods, by raiding her abode in Svarg! He has stolen her ear rings. However, I can't defeat him for he has obtained a boon from grandsire Brahma. Krishna, I appeal to you to clean the three worlds of this menace. You should do this to afford succour to the humans and the celestials. You have Sudarshan Chakra, the greatest of all weapons. And you may avail the services of Garud, the king of birds in this mission. He is keen on serving you for this purpose."

Indra had only to request and Krishna swung into action. He summoned the war council with King Ugrasen's permission.

"I am going to ride with you Krishna," his wife Satyabhama insisted on attending the meeting.

"Pragjothishyapur is far away in the east, right at the opposite end of the country. Our chariots, horses and elephants will take very long to reach there." Krishna addressed the meeting. "This is going to be an aerial operation. I shall summon the great eagle Garud and his followers. Our troops will ride the strong and large birds."

The citizens, women and children of Dwarika watched in amazement as the great Garud and flocks of his followers alighted in the large ceremonial ground when Krishna summoned them. The feathers of those birds were of various shades of brown ranging from buff, russet, amber, tan, to taupe. They had curved, sharp beaks, hooked talons and deep yellow, roving eyes.

Satyabhama, all ready in her battle outfit, was one of the first to board Garud with Krishna. Krishna, delighted by her enthusiasm, gave her a special weapon, *Shakti,* which was to be deployed by uttering a mantra.

The Yadav troops left Dwarika for Pragjothishyapur in the morning in a spectacular formation. The women's force under Satyabhama's command, dressed in colourful attire was allotted lighter birds who were at the centre. Two Yadav braves rode each large bird. Krishna sent regular reports by pigeon and hawk of their progress to the king in Dwarika. They flew over innumerable lands and crossed mountains. They Yadav braves were delighted to see the rivers Yamuna, Ganga and the mighty Brahmaputra. They marvelled at the sight of rivers pouring into the sea.

It took them half a day to reach Pragjothishyapur. Narakasur had fortified his city very well. The Yadav general Satyaki ordered one of the two riders on each of the eagles to alight at the foot of the fortress city. Krishna blew on his conch shell and the Asurs trembled on hearing its loud blare. The Yadavs laid siege to the city as soon as they dismounted. The others on the birds swept over the city and rained arrows on enemy army as the eagles emitted shrill cries. The Asurs shot back missiles at the airborne Yadavs. The foot soldiers couldn't make a dent on the exceedingly strong walls of the city of Pragjothishyapur. When the Asurs foiled several of the Yadav attempts, Krishna invoked a mantra and hurled his mace. The great walls protecting the city crumbled to dust.

Naraka's general Mura put up a fierce fight raining serpentine arrows at Krishna. An enraged Garud, with the feathers on his head standing upright, snapped at those arrows. At last Krishna used the Sudarshan Chakra to behead Mura. When Mura fell, Narakasur presented himself on the terrace of his citadel. He was immensely strong and tall with unkempt hair and fiery red eyes. Garud hovered and circled above him as Krishna showered arrows. But the arrows could not penetrate him, they bounced off his body. Naraka had a repertoire of weapons that few warriors possessed. One of his missiles struck Krishna on the forehead. Krishna swooned, slumped back and fainted.

"No man can kill me !" Narakasur laughed aloud. "I have the boon from the grandsire of the gods."

Satyabhama couldn't stand the sight of her Krishna hurt and Naraka's laughter inflamed her.

"I am no man, you fool!" she shouted back.

As Naraka prepared to launch a fatal missile on his bow an enraged Satyabhama quickly invoked the mantra and deployed the *Shakti* that Krishna had given her. It struck Naraka like lightning and went straight through his heart. Garud landed on the terrace of the palace as Naraka fell.

Satyabhama sprinkled water on Krishna and fanned him. He soon recovered.

"Narakasur is dead! I used the *Shakti* you had given me," a joyous Satyabhama said.

"You saved me! And you saved the three worlds from the atrocities of this Asur!" Krishna gave her a loving look. Satyabhama felt very happy.

The Yadav heroes gathered around them and cheered Satyabhama as well as her women's division who had fought bravely. The Asurs surrendered and the victorious Yadav troops entered the city. They saw the immense treasures Naraka had amassed there.

"Search for the earrings of Aditi," Krishna ordered. "They must be returned to the mother of gods." The Yadavs searched and found them on Naraka's person.

"Where are the women Narakasur had abducted?" Satyabhama asked.

"He has imprisoned them on Mount Mani, milady," one of Naraka's maid servants replied.

They rode the eagles and went to Mani Mountain. The prison was not a single building but a huge complex occupying the peak of that impregnable mount. The imprisoned women saw the Yadavs riding the birds from their barred windows. Loud cheers and tears of joy greeted Krishna and Satyabhama as they landed. The sight of thousands of women, many of them with babies born in captivity, kept locked in block after block of the prison was a heart-rending sight to witness. Satyabhama ordered Naraka's jailor to release the prisoners.

As locks were opened, the gates clattered and all those women gathered on the prison grounds. Standing on a platform Krishna addressed them.

"Narakasur is dead. You are free to go home!"

A woman with a baby raised her hand. "May I speak, milord?" At a nod from Krishna, she continued, "Pardon me for asking, but where will I go, my lord? Who will accept me as a wife after the beast has defiled me?"

"The Asurs killed my people and burned my house when they abducted me," another woman lamented. "I have nowhere to go."

"Don't throw us to the wolves now that you have set us free," a third one appealed.

Krishna realized that rehabilitation of these unfortunate souls, many of them mauled physically and emotionally, was a much more daunting task than liberating them. Satyabhama touched Krishna's hand and he looked at her. A silent message passed between them.

"I assure you all protection and accommodation at Dwarika as long as you wish." Krishna declared among cheers from the prisoners. From the captured chariots of the Asurs,

Krishna arranged transport and troops to escort the liberated women to Dwarika. Krishna also ordered dwellings built in Dwarika before their arrival on the west coast.

After the issue of rehabilitation of the women was settled, Krishna told Satyabhama, "Let us now visit Svarg and return the earrings to mother Aditi."

Satyabhama was excited at the prospect of visiting the much spoken about city in the Elysium. They mounted Garud again. The celestial bird took off and in no time they were way up in the sky. Mount Mani looked like a toy castle from that height. Garud flew at the speed of mind and soon they reached destination. A large city with wide roads and tall mansions loomed on the horizon. Smartly dressed young Gandharv warriors peered from the turrets of the fortification. Garud flew over them without stopping.

As they passed the gate, trumpets were blown and Indra's four-tusked, white elephant Airawat, swaying from side to side, raised its trunk above its forehead in salutation to Krishna.

"This is Svarg, lord Indra's domain." Krishna said.

Satyabhama looked at the famed realm of gods with wonderment. There was more aerial traffic as they progressed. Wonderful chariots of many shapes and sizes, bearing celestials dressed in bright, colourful raiment flew past. Some of them raised their hands in greetings. They flew over a vast garden with sprawling lawns, streams, bridges and bowers; every tree was laden with blossoms and fruits. Garud descended to a lower altitude for Satyabhama to take a good look.

"This is Nandanvan, the celestial park." Satyabhama had heard tales of the wonderful garden. She peered over the wing of Garud and saw many people of different celestial species picnicking in the park, playing games and frolicking in the lakes.

Krishna pointed towards an enormous tree with sprawling branches to their right. "See that large tree right in the centre? That's Kalpavruksha. It yields whatever a person sitting underneath it wishes for. And that great vine with little white flowers with orange stems is Parijat. Let's go closer to it," Krishna told Garud and the bird landed near the magnificent vine of thick stems.

"The vine is so wonderful," Satyabhama said caressing

its leaves.

"Rukmini has asked me to bring Parijat flowers for her," Krishna gathered flowers and holding them in his palms inhaled deeply.

"I want this vine tree, Krishna," Satyabhama's jealousy rose at the mention of Rukmini. Although Rukmini wasn't jealous of Krishna's other wives, Satyabhama was very possessive of him.

"Rukmini asked me for Parijat flowers first, Satyabhama," Krishna said mildly.

"Oh, I know you don't love me!" Satyabhama exclaimed in a gruff tone. "After I do everything for you, you love Rukmini more, I know." Her face reddened and tears welled up in her eyes.

"Come on, now, you know I do love you too!" Krishna tried to placate her. "You saved my life today, how can I forget that?"

"Then prove it! Let me have this tree," Satyabhama was adamant on her demand.

"Okay, done!" Krishna said with a smile. "I shall take it to Dwarika."

Satyabhama brightened at his words and if Garud weren't watching them, she would have kissed him.

They rode Garud again and arrived at a paved square in front of Indra's palace. Celestial citizens—deities, Gandharvs, Yakshs, Kinnars, Apsaras, Kimpurush centaurs and some eminent humans—stood there. Everybody who was somebody in Svarg was present. Garud landed at the steps and as Krishna and Satyabhama alighted, five pretty Gandharv maidens garlanded them while others showered petals. Musicians struck a sweet melody and chaperones led them up the wide marble stairs where Indra stood with open arms. He stepped forward and embraced Krishna in a brotherly hug.

Indra led them through a wide passage to his magnificent court hall. The hall was as large as the one in Dwarika. There were rows of cushioned chairs along the length and the marble covering the vast space in the middle was polished to a mirror finish. Exquisite paintings adorned the walls all around and galleries with carved railings ran around the periphery. Spiral stairways rose from the floor to the galleries at regular intervals. The high ceiling appeared to be made of translucent crystals. Colours flitted across the central dome, lending it the appearance of a rainbow. On a raised platform opposite the entrance stood the throne of the King of Deities under a white canopy supported by golden staffs.

Indra made Krishna and Satyabhama sit beside him on wide, red velvet-covered seats. A slender and pretty woman, clad in cream robes and moving gracefully, approached and greeted them.

"Meet my queen Shachi," Indra introduced his wife to Satyabhama.

"Can you take me to mother Aditi?" Satyabhama asked Shachi.

Satyabhama wanted to return the earrings they had recovered from Naraka. Shachi took Satyabhama's hand and the two of them went to Aditi.

Indra clapped and a troupe of Apsaras descended from the spiral white stairways into the well of the hall. The Gandharv and Kinnar musicians seated in the balconies played and sang while the Apsaras performed. They were damsels of renowned beauty and entertained the inmates of Svarg. Some of them were known on earth for liaisons with mortals in the past, some sent on specific missions to earth by the lord of Svarg. The dance and the accompanying song kept Krishna enthralled.

By the time the song ended and the troupe had left among applause, Shachi returned with Satyabhama.

"Look what mother Aditi gave me!" Satyabhama showed the gifts Aditi had given her.

"We would like to have the Parijat vine in Dwarika," Krishna told Indra remembering the gift his wives wanted.

Indra looked at Queen Shachi. Imperceptibly she shook her head, indicating a 'no.' Indra did not want to part with *Parijat* either.

"Well, you know the ladies in Svarg love the tree," Indra said. Although he was grateful for the defeat of Naraka, he had not forgotten his humiliation by Krishna in the Mount Govardhan and Khandav fire affairs. "We can't give you the vine, but we shall provide many amenities for Dwarika as you have rid the three worlds from the menace of Naraka."

Krishna and Satyabhama took leave of Indra. On the way

back Krishna simply took the vine, although Indra had refused to give it. They rode Garud and returned to Dwarika.

In a grand ceremony King Ugrasen honoured Krishna. Krishna distributed the riches obtained from Pragjothishyapur among the braves belonging to all the Yadav tribes. He honoured Garud and bid him farewell.

When Krishna went to his palace from the assembly, Satyabhama rushed to him. "Let's place the Parijat tree in my courtyard," she said.

"Yes, of course. Where would you like it to be placed?"

"Umm... place it near the hedge," she pointed to the hedge next to Rukmini's courtyard. Krishna merely smiled; he understood that Satyabhama wanted to make Rukmini jealous.

"Sure," Krishna smiled and directed the gardener to plant the thick stemmed vine tree of Parijat at the spot Satyabhama had pointed. "Happy?"

"I love you so, Krishna," Satyabhama said.

Next morning Krishna visited Rukmini. She welcomed him with handfuls of Parijat flowers. "Thank you, Krishna for the flowers," she said. Krishna looked at her courtyard and saw that although the tree was in Satyabhama's courtyard the early morning breeze had blown all the flowers into Rukmini's courtyard.

"You wanted the Parijat flowers, and you got them." A broad smile adorned Krishna's face. "Satyabhama wanted the tree, and she got it. Each one gets what they ask for."

Although Indra was quite upset that Krishna took away the *Parijat,* he kept his word and soon enough Vishwakarma, the celestial architect, arrived in Dwarika. He built sparkling lakes abundant with lilies and lotuses of various colours. He populated them with spectacular aquatic creatures of various kinds. He inlaid the columns of Dwarika's gates with precious jewels. He planted the parks with trees of multi-coloured leaves and flowers. Peacocks and birds with coloured feathers dotted the wide lawns. He decorated the steps of palaces with gold. He laid marble tiles in the squares of Dwarika.

Soon the caravan of the rescued women arrived from Pragjothishyapur. The women became the responsibility of the

Yadav state. They were housed in comfortable quarters that Krishna had asked Vishwakarma to build. Krishna arranged for their livelihood. Thus he came to be known as the 'husband of sixteen thousand wives.'

12. Justice for Jarasandh

Although Krishna returned to Dwarika, he was keenly interested in the developments in Indraprasth. Yudhisthir and he often sent messengers informing each other of their wellbeing.

Krishna learned that along with the Asur Maya, whom Arjun had rescued from the forest fire, arrived a huge contingent of *Yakshs* and *Rakshas*. They were demonic soldiers, who guarded the palace while under construction. Maya worked on it ceaselessly, day and night. The building was kept hidden from all human eyes.

At the end of fourteen months of building, Maya was satisfied with his creation. On an auspicious day, Yudhisthir followed by his brothers, wife, and mother entered it after due rites. The whole place was bathed in effulgence which was a mixture of tastefully arranged colourful celestial and terrestrial lights. The palace that the dexterous Maya built was composed of excellent materials, furnished with golden walls and archways. Adorned with varied pictures it was withal so rich and well-built, that in beauty it far surpassed the palace of Brahma himself. A hundred fierce demons, capable of ranging through the air, guarded and protected the palace. Within that palace Maya had placed a peerless tank in which he placed lotuses with leaves of dark-coloured gems and stalks of bright jewels, and other flowers of golden leaves. Aquatic fowl of various species sported on its bosom. Variegated with full-blown lotuses and stocked with fish and tortoises of golden hue, its bottom was without mud and its water transparent. There was a flight of crystal stairs leading from the banks to the edge of the water. The gentle breezes that swept along its bosom swayed the flowers that studded it. The banks of that tank were overlaid with slabs of expensive marble set with pearls. Beholding that tank adorned all around with jewels and precious stones, many guests mistook it for land and fell into it. Maya built another tank in another passage in which were embedded polished marbles of various colours, so it appeared like a water pool. Many visitors were fooled and lifted their attire to prevent them from getting wet while crossing it. There were doors which turned out to be solid walls when one tried to pass through them and what appeared like walls at certain places were in reality doors and people fell through them.

All around the palace, trees of various kinds were planted that were all very charming to behold. Artificial woods were laid around, always emitting a delicious fragrance. There were many tanks that were adorned with swans and *Brahminy* ducks in the grounds lying about the mansion. Breeze bearing the fragrance of lotuses growing in water and those growing on land ministered unto the pleasure and happiness of the residents and visitors of Indraprasth. Numerous guests from all walks of life visited the city every day to see this wonder. Word of the splendour of the palace spread far and wide and so did the fame of King Yudhisthir and his brothers.

In due course, Subhadra became a proud mother of Arjun's son they named Abhimanyu. Right from childhood he became a favourite of Krishna and his uncles. Abhimanyu acquired from his father the science of weapons, celestial, and human. The child also acquired the knowledge of counteracting the weapons hurled at him by others, and great lightness of hand and fleetness of chariot motions forward and backward and transverse, and wheeling.

Draupadi bore a son each to her five husbands. They were born at intervals of one year that each brother stayed with Draupadi according to their mutual agreement. All the sons of the Pandavs grew together and were quite attached and fond of each other. They received training from their fathers and uncles in respective fields of their expertise.

The Pandavs spent several peaceful years ruling the land of their forefathers with wisdom and justice. Yudhisthir paid attention to virtue, pleasure, and profit in equal proportion. He treated his citizens of all classes with equality. The disparity in the riches of the subjects did not attain extreme proportions and everybody had enough and more to live on. Citizens grew and prospered like souls in a happy body. Their properties were well-protected and citizens lived without fear of robbers. They admired and respected their king, but did not fear him. The Pandavs became a topic of discussion in social and political circles all over Aryavart. Yudhisthir's just rule became a subject of admiration for many kings and of jealousy for some.

One fine day messengers from Yudhisthir arrived to the island city of Dwarika inviting Krishna for consultation on an important issue that was being discussed with some fervour in Indraprasth.

"I am advised by friends and counsellors to perform the *Rajsuya* sacrifice, and to assume the title of Emperor," Yudhisthir explained to Krishna when he arrived in the magnificent palace built by Maya. "But that is not something which happens by mere wishing. Some advisors do not see the difficulties due to close friendship; some, from motives of self-interest say only what is agreeable. Krishna, you are above all this and I trust that the advice you will afford will be in the best of interest of all concerned."

"Yes of course, I will tell you what I think," Krishna said, "but before I do so, I would like to know what you think on the subject."

"I am quite content with ruling Indraprasth," Yudhisthir spoke. "I would prefer peaceful relations among all kingdoms to attainment of imperial dignity. If man does not control by moderation, his desires know no bound. I regard peace of mind as the highest object on earth, for from that quality alone I may attain the satisfaction of living a good life."

"It has been seen," Bheem spoke after Yudhisthir had his say, "that even a king who is weaker in military strength may vanquish an enemy who is strong by the firm belief in his abilities. I believe that a *Kshatriya* warrior should not lead a life of inaction devoid of courage and valour. When I get old, then I will wear saffron clothes and retire to the forest to spend time chanting the Lord's name, but when we are young and full of energy we must fulfil our desires by exercising all our faculties. I feel that the King should perform the *Rajsuya* and bring all the kings of the land under his aegis."

When they had stopped speaking, Krishna cleared his throat and the others leaned forward in their seats, eager to know his opinion.

"The stature of an emperor is not to be desired as a means to attain personal glory or obtain wealth," he said, "on the contrary, one has to rise in stature to attain the title. It is not military superiority, but respect from other kings, which makes a king worthy of this high stature. When all kings in a country are under the aegis of a worthy emperor, peace reigns in that land. It is a process of unification, which augurs progress. The weakest king also rests assured that the emperor will protect his people from aggressors and support them in calamities like endemic diseases, locusts, flood or draughts. When kings are secure, they concentrate their attention on development of their populace rather than war among themselves. Peace facilitates commerce and exchange of wealth among people.

"If anyone is worthy of the title of an emperor in Aryavart today it is you, King Yudhisthir, precisely because you do not desire it. You have gained a unique reputation of being just in your rule, treating all classes of citizens with unbiased equality, and almost all the kings will be happy to accept your leadership if you send them an invitation to attend the *Rajsuya Yadnya*.

"Moreover, if virtuous and capable persons desist from assuming leadership—either from lack of ambition or from motives of spirituality—the greedy and the cruel rush to fill the void in leadership and the populace suffer untold miseries under them, for they grind the weak from unabashed selfish motives. Today the only one capable of challenging King Yudhisthir's claim to lead the kings is one such wicked king, King Jarasandh of Magadh. He has raised a huge army and has already begun his campaign of subjugating neighbouring kings forcefully. There is none in Aryavart today capable of facing his colossal war designs. That wicked fellow is planning to sacrifice a hundred human kings to please Rudra, the Lord of Destruction. He has already captured and imprisoned eighty-four kings. After he completes this human sacrifice, he will come into possession of unrivalled powers and embark on his conquest of Aryavart with renewed vigour."

"Krishna," Yudhisthir said, "I appreciate your views and have understood that the performance of *Rajsuya* is not for gratifying personal ambition, but to provide leadership. However, you also speak of the military capabilities of King Jarasandh who is vying for the title of emperor. How can the

Rajsuya be performed without war?"

"I am a firm believer in avoiding war unless inevitable, for it brings untold miseries to the population of both parties. Death, disease, and destitution afflict even the land of the conqueror," Krishna said. "However, there are some factors which can make it possible to defeat King Jarasandh without waging a war. Firstly, Jarasandh is facing a temporary setback because the Yadavs have eliminated his strong ally and son-in-law Kans and his two dauntless generals have, of late, committed suicide due to some misunderstanding. Secondly, Jarasandh has his own code of morality born out of vanity. After his evening worship, he distributes alms to *Brahmins* and never refuses any alms that a *Brahmin* might ask of him. He also prides himself, and indeed, he is one of the greatest living wrestlers proficient in unarmed combat. If we can bypass his forces and reach him to challenge him to a duel, he will accept the challenge out of pride.

"I propose that I, along with Bheem and Arjun, approach him and challenge him to a duel. If we defeat him, we can release the eighty-four princes he has imprisoned and they all will be happy to accept your leadership. Luckily, Jarasandh's son does not share the vile ambition of his father and he will rule his kingdom peacefully. This way we can avoid a war and its undesirable effects and you can perform the *Rajsuya Yadnya* comfortably. But if you falter now, sooner or later the mighty host of Jarasandh will be knocking on the gates of Indraprasth and war will become inevitable.

"Jarasandh's forces can't be vanquished in the battlefield even by all the celestials and the trolls fighting together. I think, however, that he can be vanquished in a one-on-one unarmed combat. In me is policy, in Bheem is strength and in Arjun is triumph; and therefore, as prelude to performing the *Rajsuya*, we will achieve the destruction of the ruler of Magadh. If you have any faith in me, make over to me, as a pledge, Bheem and Arjun!"

"Krishna," Yudhisthir exclaimed, "You are the lord of us Pandavs and I have explicit and full faith in your judgment. Moreover, I see that Bheem and Arjun are eager to undertake this mission by your side. I consider Jarasandh as already slain, the eighty-four kings already set free and the *Rajsuya* already performed."

The three travellers from Indraprasth arrived at the ring formed by the five mountains. They rested for a breather on the shoulder of the southern hill. The magnificent city of Magadh nestled in the bowl of valley formed by those five hills. Green fields, pastures, and innumerable trees provided a pleasant backdrop to the bright and high structures dominating the city.

Krishna, Bheem, and Arjun had travelled for almost a fortnight, crossing numerous rivers, lakes, and hills. They rested atop the hills overlooking the capital of King Jarasandh, admiring that magnificent city.

"I must tell you an important piece of information about Jarasandh," Krishna told Bheem and Arjun while they waited. "Jarasandh's father was a noble soul and a great warrior. He had married two princesses from the kingdom of Kashi and treated both queens equally in all respects. Since neither of the queens bore children, the King approached a renowned sage and prayed for a remedy. The sage was sitting underneath a mango tree and as Jarasandh's father spoke, a mango fell down in the sage's hand. The sage offered the mango to the King, asking him to give it to the queen. He assured that the queen would bear a child after consuming that mango.

"With a desire to be fair to both his queens, the King cut the mango vertically into two halves and gave one half to each. In due course, the queens became pregnant, but they delivered only one half of a child each. Horrified at the ghastly sight, they asked their midwives to throw away the baby halves. The two midwives threw each half away from each other at the corner of the lane behind the palace.

"An old giantess was passing that way and when she saw the pieces of flesh, she picked them up, wanting to eat them and as she brought the two pieces together by accident, they joined and life appeared in the baby. The giantess was moved by the sight of the new-born baby and took it to the queens. The queens with their bosoms full of milk were delighted and received their child with joy." Krishna told them. "The child, a son, was named Jarasandh, meaning "joined by the old giantess." Bear this in mind while fighting with Jarasandh that he has this weakness where he was joined in the centre of his body."

After resting for some time, the trio descended the slope into the valley. They were dressed in simple white attire and did not carry any weapons. They reached the town as dusk began to settle on the land. They did not enter by the main gates of the city, but by one of the side gates. The citizens saw them and took them for *Brahmins,* and looking at their majestic bearing, wondered who they could be as they proceeded towards the palace along streets lit with oil lamps mounted on tall posts.

When the three reached the brightly lit palace, the King was busy with his evening prayers. Earlier, Jarasandh's chief priest had had premonitions, so rituals had been performed to ward off the imminent danger. The King was made to mount an elephant and lighted brands were whirled about him. A number of *Brahmins* were waiting and when the rituals were over Jarasandh presented them with gifts. The trio from Indraprasth were the last in the queue.

"What may I offer you, revered ones?" Jarasandh asked of them with folded hands.

"These two friends of mine have taken a vow of silence, your majesty," Krishna replied, "they can speak only after midnight."

"So be it," the King said, "let them rest; I shall meet them at midnight."

They were led to the guesthouse, where they waited. They rested until midnight, when King Jarasandh visited them as promised. He noticed that although they were wearing the attire of *Brahmins,* their hands bore marks of the bowstring and unlike *Brahmins,* they had smeared sandalwood paste on their bodies.

"You have come to me as *Brahmins* but I have reports that you entered the city by the wrong gate," Jarasandh asked them, "Why did you not accept my worship? Who are you and why have you come here?"

"We don the white attire of students," Krishna replied, "We came by the wrong gate to make you aware of our intentions, which are to warn you and challenge you if you don't heed our warning."

"You dare to warn a king in his own palace!" Jarasandh

was more amused than angry. "And why would you warn me? I have done you no harm; in fact I do not remember having met you before."

"I am Krishna and these are the sons of King Pandu, Bheem and Arjun. You have harmed our brethren—the eighty-four kings whom you have imprisoned. We warn you, desist from the human sacrifice you are planning. We urge you to release those kings forthwith."

"Oh, so you are Krishna! You are the one who killed Kans my son in-law!" Jarasandh examined Krishna from head to toe. "I have conquered those kings after defeating them in battle and I shall not let anyone come in the way of my proposed sacrifice. Now spare me the speech on morality and ask of me what you have come to ask. I always grant the wishes of those who ask after my evening prayer." Jarasandh spoke with pride.

"We desire an unarmed duel to the death with you," Krishna said.

"You ask foolishly," Jarasandh said, "do you not know that none has ever defeated me in a wrestling match?"

"You may choose any one of us." Krishna ignored his boast.

"Well, I have warned you." Jarasandh looked at Krishna, Bheem, and Arjun sizing them up. He pointed at Bheem. "I choose this one. At least he possesses sturdy physique. My servants will come to fetch you when the preparations for the match are complete."

Jarasandh left them duly impressed by his magnanimity in granting the wish of even those who had come to challenge him.

Krishna asked Bheem to get some sleep, for he knew it would be a long fight. Jarasandh summoned his ministers and ordered them to get the ground ready for the duel. He sent for his masseur and physician. Jarasandh removed his crown and tied his hair. He donned the short attire, discarding his robes and girded his loins. They massaged the King's body with ointments for speedy recovery from injuries. The physician administered potions that would help in quick revival if he were to fall unconscious during the fight.

Word of the impending duel spread like wild fire and people crowded the wrestling stadium in the city of Magadh. All the seats were occupied long before the match began.

Those who could not obtain a seat climbed atop trees and tall buildings near the stadium in the hope of witnessing the action. The King's son, ministers and generals occupied prominent seats in the front, while Krishna and Arjun sat on the opposite side of the ring.

"Jarasandh is very powerful and skilled," Krishna whispered a last minute tip to Bheem as the latter prepared to enter the arena, "but he is older than you by several years. Try to tire him out, only then will you be able to dominate him."

The two combatants entered and stood in the centre of the vast ring; they possessed no other weapon than their bare arms. Their muscular, oiled bodies glowed in the early morning sun. Bheem was somewhat taller, while Jarasandh's broad shoulders conveyed immense strength. They performed the statutory salutation. They slapped their armpits, causing the enclosure to tremble at the sound. The spectators held their breath as Bheem and Jarasandh circled each other. They stared into each other's eyes trying to read when the other would make the first move. At last they rushed towards each other in unison and locked their hands around the opponent's neck, and the duel was underway. They seized arms and twined each other's legs in an attempt to bring the other down. They pushed and dragged each other violently. They raised their arms, feigning, and then dropped to get hold of the other's limbs. They kicked hard at chosen points to damage the nerves within. They roared and struck each other in the chest with clenched fists. With sudden jerks, they lifted the other high above the ground and threw him down. They were evenly matched in their expertise in different holds and manoeuvres to escape those holds.

Bheem realized what Krishna had told him, it was not possible to defeat Jarasandh quickly. He started fighting with a defensive stance, letting Jarasandh take the offensive. Bheem parried when Jarasandh struck, ducked under blows, and jumped up when Jarasandh tried to kick at his legs. He smothered jabs, but he also attacked in between, so Jarasandh did not get too close. The fight continued through noon to evening. Bheem felt Jarasandh's strength waning after they had fought non-stop for almost ten hours. Jarasandh's reactions were getting slower and he paused a fraction more between his charges.

Bheem glanced at Krishna who was holding a blade of grass in his hands. As their eyes met, Krishna tore the blade vertically.

Bheem attacked Jarasandh feigning to the right, then swerving at the last minute he slid along the ground and kicked Jarasandh's legs out from under him. Jarasandh collapsed and in a flash Bheem was on top of him. He pressed down his left foot on Jarasandh's right leg and holding the other leg in his hands, he heaved with all his might. A blood-curdling cry emanated from Jarasandh. With the terrifying sound of tearing tissues and cracking bones, Jarasandh's body split in two vertical halves. Bheem let out a roar of triumph and threw down the half from his hands. Bheem's cry ended as he watched in horror the two halves join back together. Jarasandh was up again and his raucous laughter shook the stadium. The audience was dumbstruck at the hair-raising sight.

Krishna was trying to draw Bheem's attention but an infuriated Bheem attacked Jarasandh again with ferocity and rent him asunder, but once again Jarasandh rose laughing as soon as the severed halves of his body hit the ground. A flabbergasted Bheem looked at Krishna who was still holding the two pieces of the blade of grass he had torn before; as soon as their eyes met, he crossed his hands and threw the piece in his right hand to his left and the left to the right.

Bheem attacked Jarasandh, ripped his body in two yet again and cast the halves apart so that the exposed and bloody sides faced away from one another. Everybody waited with breath abated. Minutes passed by, but this time the two halves of Jarasandh's body remained apart.

In the dead silence that ensued, Jarasandh's son approached Krishna with folded hands.

"You don't have to bow to me. You are now the King of Magadh and free to rule your land as you please," Krishna said, "We only desire that the eighty-four kings imprisoned by your father Jarasandh be released."

Jarasandh's son ordered the release of the eighty-four kings from prison and they all followed Krishna out of the city, where they assembled on a vast ground. They thanked Krishna and the two Pandavs. Krishna advised them about Yudhisthir's proposed *Rajsuya* sacrifice and they offered to support him in every respect in this endeavour.

"I would like permission to perform the last rites of my father," Jarasandh's son told Krishna.

"You do not need anybody's permission, your majesty," Krishna assured him. He knew that enough time had lapsed and the tissues were dead and Jarasandh could never be revived again, even if the two pieces were joined for the funeral.

After the cremation, Jarasandh's ministers requested Krishna to crown the dead King's son and Krishna obliged them. The new king entered his city and all the liberated kings returned to their respective kingdoms with great joy, praising Krishna and the Pandav brothers.

13. Shenanigans of Shishupal

With Jarasandh gone, fervent preparations began in Indraprasth for the *Rajsuya* sacrifice. Quarters were made ready for housing the guests in the shining palace built by Maya with wide passages, stairs and entrances. It was equipped with luxurious furniture, wall hangings and exotic carpets. Large quantities of excellent foods and wines were bought and stored. All the materials required for the *yadnya* were procured as advised by the sages. The streets were illuminated and decorated. Citizens painted their houses.

Soon, Yudhisthir's messengers riding swift mounts were dispatched with invitations to all the kingdoms. As the assigned day for the Rajsuya drew near, royal visitors from all over Aryavart started arriving at Indraprasth. Balram and other Yadav braves from Dwarika were among the first to arrive. King Dhrutarashtra came with his entourage of Bhishm, Vidur, Duryodhan and his brothers, along with Karn and the preceptors Krupa and Dron along with his son Ashwatthama. King Jaidrath the ruler of Sindhu, brother in law to Duryodhan arrived with them. The King of Gandhar Suvala arrived with Prince Shakuni and his brothers. King Shalya, uncle to Nakul and Sahdev and brother to their mother Madri, arrived from Madra with his ministers. The king of the Mleccha tribes from the western seashore, the kings of the Malavs and the Andhraks; and the Dravids and the Singhals, the King of Kashmir, and King Kuntibhoj arrived with their tributes. Innumerable kings arrived from the middle lands and from inaccessible hilly regions and marshy lands of the East.

On the appointed day, Yudhisthir prepared for the *Rajsuya yadnya* under the guidance of Sage Vyas and with the help of his innumerable benefactors. Bhishm and Dron supervised the overall arrangements. Vidur supervised the distribution of gifts to *Brahmins* and all those who attended the *yadnya* while Krishna engaged in receiving all the sages. Duryodhan took over the responsibility of receiving the tributes offered by each ruler. Desirous of looking at that sacrificial mansion, and Emperor Yudhisthir the Just, none came there with tribute less than a thousand in number, weight or measure.

The sacrificial compound of the illustrious son of Kunti looked impressive with the multitude of palaces built to last forever and crowded with guards and warriors. These were so high that their tops touched the chariots of the gods who came to behold that sacrifice. The citizens looked on with awe as god after god arrived in wonderful chariots, the likes of which were never seen before on earth.

As gifts Yudhisthir received hundreds of green horses of a species possessing noses like parrots, camels and she-asses, goats and kine. Kings from afar presented rare vegetables, honey and jewels and gems of various kinds. One king brought him a tribute of innumerable skins—black, darkish and red, of the rarest of rare deer. Others brought a tribute of numberless blankets of excellent textures inlaid with gold; swords with handles made of the purest ivory and adorned with diamonds; armours of diverse hues decked with jewels and gold and ivory; chariots of various shapes and handsome make with well trained horses trimmed with tiger skins and long swords and scimitars, and hatchets and fine-edged battle-axes manufactured in the western countries. Another gave ten thousand asses of large size and black necks and capable of running two hundred miles every day. Tribal men brought with them as tribute, large elephants and variegated blankets for caparisoning elephants. They who dwell by the side of the rivers brought as tribute a heaping of rare gold, measured in jars, raised from underneath the earth by ants. The mountain tribes brought as tribute numerous umbrellas: soft and black and white. The forest dwelling Kirat Kings brought as tribute loads upon loads of sandal and aloe—also black aloe. The Deity of Ocean himself brought, in vessels of white copper, the nectar that is generated within his waters and which is much superior to that which flowers and annual plants produce.

When all the preparations were complete, the *yadnya* began at an auspicious time.

Then grandsire Bhishm, the eldest of the Kurus and uncle to the Pandavs, addressing King Yudhisthir the Just, said, "Let

Arghya —the article of respect—be offered unto the kings as each of them deserves. And let an *Arghya* be presented first of all unto him among those present who is the foremost."

"O Grandsire, whom do you deem the foremost amongst these assembled and unto whom the *Arghya* should be presented by us, please tell me," Yudhisthir requested.

"Krishna is the foremost of all. He shines among us all like a sun and illuminates our world, let the article of respect be offered to him first," Bhishm replied.

The Pandavs duly presented the first *Arghya* of excellent ingredients unto the Yadav Krishna of the Vrishni race. Krishna also accepted it according to the forms of the ordinance. But Shishupal could not bear to see that worship offered to Krishna. This King of Chedi was opposed to Krishna from the beginning. He was a protégé of Jarasandh and had participated in the campaign against Mathura. It was he with whom Rukmini's marriage was fixed, when she eloped with Krishna. He bore a grudge against Krishna for slaying his benefactor Jarasandh.

"This Krishna of the Vrishni clan does not deserve royal worship as if he were a king, in the midst of all these illustrious monarchs," reproving both Bhishm and Yudhisthir, Shishupal censured Krishna. "You sons of Pandu, this conduct of yours in thus willingly worshipping him is not worthy of the illustrious Pandavs. You are mere children. You know not what is proper conduct, for that is very subtle.

"And you Bhishm, although advanced in age, you are of little knowledge and transgressed the rules of morality. You have offered ill advice to the Pandavs out of motives of interest and you deserve to be censured too. The first *Arghya* is to be offered to one who is either a king, or revered due to knowledge, or is an elderly person or a great warrior. Krishna is neither a sacrificial priest nor a preceptor, nor a king.

"Tell me, how this Krishna, who is not a king, can be worshipped when great kings are present here? Bypassing greats like King Bhishmak of Vidarbha, or King Dhrutarashtra of Hastinapur or King Drupad of the Panchals is an insult to those royals. Does this Krishna possess more knowledge than the sages present here? Bypassing Sage Narad, or Sage Vyas is an insult to those great sages. This Krishna is not a great warrior either. Bypassing such heroes as Balram, or Karn, or Ashwatthama, or Duryodhan is an insult to them. Then again, is this Krishna so advanced in age that he deserves to be worshipped? It is an insult to King Ugrasen and Krishna's own father Vasudev. How can a son be worshipped when the father is here? Why, Bhishm, you are yourself the eldest of the Kurus, King Yudhisthir should have offered the first *Arghya* to you!

"Why were these monarchs brought here to be insulted thus? We have not paid tributes to the illustrious son of Kunti from fear, from desire of gain, or from having been won over by conciliation. On the other hand, we have paid him tribute simply because he has been desirous of the imperial dignity from motives of virtue. And yet he it is that thus insults us. O king, from what else, save motives of insult, could it have been that you have worshipped Krishna, who possesses not the insignia of royalty, with the *Arghya* in the midst of the assembled monarchs? Indeed, the reputation for virtue that Yudhisthir, the just, has acquired, has been acquired by him without cause, for who would offer such undue worship unto one that has fallen off from virtue. This wretch born in the race of the Vrishnis by cunning slew the illustrious King Jarasandh. Righteousness has today been abandoned by Yudhisthir and meanness only has been displayed by him in consequence of his having offered the *Arghya* to Krishna.

"And you Krishna, don't you have sense enough to guide the naive Pandavs when they are being misguided by Bhishm? How shamelessly you accepted the *Arghya*! You are like a dog who quietly sits in a corner lapping up stolen sacrificial butter. In fact, it is not an insult offered to the monarchs by the Pandavs, but to you. Krishna, as a wife is to one that is without virile power, as a fine show is to one that is blind, so is this royal worship to you who are no king. What Yudhisthir is, has been seen; what Bhishm is, has been seen; and what this Krishna is has been seen. Indeed, all these have been seen as they are!"

With these words of insult to Bhishm, the Pandavs and Krishna Shishupal got up from his seat and urged the kings present there to boycott King Yudhisthir's sacrifice. Yudhisthir hastily ran after Shishupal and spoke unto him sweetly and in a conciliating tone.

"What you have said is scarcely proper for the occasion. O King of Chedi, it is highly sinful and needlessly cruel. Insult not

Bhishm by saying that he doth not know what virtue is. Behold, these many kings, older than you, all approve of the worship offered unto Krishna. It behoves you to bear it patiently like them. O ruler of Chedi, Bhishm knows Krishna truly.

"We have offered Krishna the first worship because of his fame, his heroism, his success. Indeed, liberality, cleverness, knowledge of the Vedas, bravery, modesty, achievements, excellent intelligence, humility, beauty, firmness, contentment and prosperity—all dwell Krishna. He is the foremost in all the worlds including the regions of the celestials."

"If Shishupal does not approve the worship offered unto Krishna, the oldest one in the universe, he deserves neither soft words nor conciliation," Bhishm spoke to Yudhisthir. "This Shishupal is a mere boy and hence he knows not Krishna, and ever and everywhere speaks wrongly of Krishna. This ruler of Chedi will never see virtue in that light in which one that is desirous of acquiring high merit will see it. Who is there among the old and the young or among these illustrious lords of earth that does not regard Krishna as deserving of worship or that does not worship Krishna? If Shishupal regards this worship as undeserved, let him go away and leave us in peace."

"Old and infamous wretch of the Kurus, are you not ashamed of asking me to leave!" Shishupal flared up. "You are living a life of celibacy and are honoured but how can you give such counsel that is so wide of morality. Like a boat tied to another boat or the blind following the blind, are the Kurus who have you for their guide. Arrogant and ignorant as you are why does not this tongue of yours split up into a hundred parts? How do you desire to praise that cow-boy in respect of whom even men of little intelligence may address invectives? If Krishna in his infancy slew a wet nurse, what is there remarkable in that? What is there remarkable in this one's having lifted the Govardhan mount, which is like an anthill? What is so great in his subjugating Kalia, who is like a wriggling worm? What is so great in his slaying Naraka, who had done Krishna no harm? But, you who should be conversant with the rules of morality, is not this still more wrongful that Krishna slew Kans, whose food he ate? Who will regard as praiseworthy the act which was done by Krishna in the matter of Jarasandh's death? He made the Pandavs enter by an improper gate, disguised as a Brahman. You, Bhishm, infamous one of the Kuru race, you are ignorant of the rules of morality. Womanish in disposition and bent down with age, you feign celibacy but are in fact an impotent wretch!"

Then Sage Narad clad in black deer-skin, upset on hearing Shishupal's rant, admonished him, "Those men that will not worship the lotus-eyed Krishna should be regarded as dead though alive, and should never be talked to on any occasion. Either behave or go away Shishupal from here."

Bheem also became very angry on hearing Shishupal unjustly insulting Bhishm. His eyes turned red under the influence of that rage. When Bheem began to grind his teeth in rage, the monarchs beheld his face resembling that of Death himself, at the end of the Yuga, prepared to swallow every creature. And as the hero endued with great energy was about to leap up impetuously, the mighty-armed Bhishm caught him and restrained him with various kinds of counsel. Shishupal laughed at Bheem and said to Bhishm, "Release him, old man! Let all the monarchs behold him scorched by my prowess like an insect in fire."

"Don't heed his words, Bheem," Bhishm said, "let Krishna handle him. This Shishupal is a younger maternal cousin of Krishna. There is a reason why Krishna has not punished him all this time. Let me tell you about it.

> "Shishupal was born in the line of Chedis. He had three eyes and four hands when he was born. As soon as he was born, he screamed and brayed like an ass. On that account his father and mother, along with their relatives, were struck with fear. And beholding these extraordinary omens his parents resolved to abandon him. But an incorporeal voice said unto the king and his wife with hearts paralysed by anxiety, those words, 'This your son, O king, that has been born will survive and become superior in strength. Therefore you have no fear from him. Indeed cherish the child without anxiety. He will not die in childhood. His time is not yet come. He that will slay him with weapons has also been born.' Hearing these words, the mother, rendered anxious by affection for her son, addressed the invisible Being and said, 'I bow with

joined hands unto him that has uttered these words respecting my son; whether he be an exalted divinity or any other being, let him tell me another word, I desire to hear who will be the slayer of this my son.' The invisible Being then said, 'He upon whose lap this child being placed the superfluous arms of his will fall down upon the ground, and at the sight of whom his third eye on the forehead will disappear, will be his slayer.' Hearing of the child's three eyes and four arms as also of the words of the invisible Being, all the kings of the earth went to Chedi to behold the child. The king of Chedi gave his child upon their laps one after another. And though the child was placed upon the laps of a hundred kings, one after another, yet that which the incorporeal voice had said came not to pass. And having heard of all this at Dwarika, the Yadav heroes Balram and Krishna also went to the capital of the Chedis, to see their father's sister—the queen of Chedi. Saluting the king and queen, and enquiring after everybody's welfare, Balram and Krishna took their seats. And after those heroes had been received, the queen herself placed the child on the lap of Krishna. As soon as the child was placed on his lap, those superfluous arms of his fell down and the eye on his forehead also disappeared.

"Having seen this, the queen in alarm and anxiety begged of Krishna a boon. 'Krishna, my dear nephew, I am afflicted with fear for my child; grant me a boon.'

"'Fear not, dear aunty,' Krishna replied. 'Have no fear from me. What boon shall I give you? What shall I do?'

"Thus spoken to by Krishna, the queen said, 'You have to pardon the offences of Shishupal for my sake. This is the boon that I ask.'

"Krishna then said, 'Dear aunty, even when he will deserve to be punished, I will pardon a hundred offences of his. Please don't grieve.'

"This is why Krishna keeps silent over this wretched being's misdeeds."

On hearing Bhishm's words, Shishupal became agitated.

"This wretched Bhishm, though old, is exceedingly boastful. He deserves not our pardon. Therefore, all you kings, it is well that this wretch were slain like an animal, or, mustering together, let us burn him in a fire of grass or straw."

The whole assembly was shocked to see Shishupal adopt such a belligerent stance.

"O Krishna," Shishupal shrieked at the top of his voice, "I challenge you. Come, fight with me until I slay you today with all the Pandavs."

When the event turned so violent, Krishna addressing all the kings spoke calmly, "This wicked-minded one, though the son of a daughter of the Yadav race, is a great enemy of us. Though we never seek to injure him, he ever seeks our evil. This rascal of cruel deeds, hearing that we had gone to the city of Pragjothishyapur, came and attacked Dwarika, although he is the son of my father's sister. While king Ugrasen was sporting on the Raivatak hill, this one fell upon the attendants of that king and slew and led away many of them in chains to his own city. Sinful in all his purpose, this caitiff, in order to obstruct the sacrifice of my father, stole the sacrificial horse that had been let loose. Prompted by sinful motives, this one ravished the reluctant wife of the innocent Akrur on her way from Dwarika to her parents' city. This injurer of his maternal uncle, disguising himself in the attire of a king ravished the innocent Bhadra, the princess of Visala, the intended bride of King Karusha. This fool had desired Rukmini and wanted to marry her against her will. I have patiently borne all these offences for the sake of my father's sister. It is, however, very fortunate that all this has occurred today in the presence of all the kings. Behold you all today the hostility this one bears towards me. And know also all that he has done me at my back. For the excess of that pride in which he has indulged in the presence of all these monarchs, he deserves to be punished by me. This is his hundredth offence. I am ill able to pardon today the injuries that he has done me, the Pandavs and the Kurus. He wants to tarnish the image of the just king Yudhisthir by disrupting his *Rajsuya*."

Hearing these words of Krishna, many of the assembled monarchs began to reprove the ruler of Chedi. But Shishupal, boastful as he was, having heard these words, laughed aloud and said, "Krishna, are you not ashamed in saying in this assembly, especially before all these kings that your wife Rukmini had been coveted by me? Who else other than you, who regarding himself a man would say in the midst of respectable men that his wife had been coveted by somebody else? O Krishna, pardon me if you please, or pardon me not. But I shall not let this sacrifice be fulfilled."

He turned to all the assembled kings. "When I am here to head you all, what are ye thinking of now? Arrayed let us stand in battle against the assembled Yadavs and the Pandavs!"

Some of the invited monarchs, who bore a grudge against the Kurus or Yadavs joined him. Though their friends sought to appease them, their faces glowed with anger like those of roaring lions driven away from their prey. Krishna then understood that these monarchs with countless waves of troops were preparing for a terrific rush. And while Shishupal was preparing to attack, Krishna thought in his mind of the discus that had humbled the pride of the Asurs. As soon as the discus came into his hands, Krishna uttered these words aloud, "Listen you lords of earth, as promised to his mother, a hundred offences of Shishupal were to be pardoned by me. He has completed one hundred offences. I shall not tolerate his challenge to me and the Pandavs."

The celestial disc rose from Krishna's hand and whirring in air, the missile instantly cut off the head of the ruler of Chedi. As the villain fell down like a cliff struck with thunder, the discus returned to Krishna.

In the stunned silence that followed, Krishna said to King Yudhisthir, "There is no enmity with the dead. Let him be given a decent funeral with proper respect deserving his status. Let his son be installed with due ceremony on the throne of Chedi."

With the threat of Shishupal removed King Yudhisthir's great *Rajsuya* was completed. The assembled great sages, celestial and kings with pleased hearts praised Krishna and the Pandavs and went away.

14. The War at Dwarika

Having successfully completed the *Rajsuya* of the Pandavs, Krishna was on his way to Dwarika with Satyabhama. His sister Subhadra and her son Abhimanyu had also joined them. Balram and Satyaki were in a car behind them. Their train of chariots left Indraprasth and was a short distance away from the city, when they saw a messenger gallop from the opposite direction. Krishna's charioteer stopped the vehicle. Balram and Satyaki came over too. The messenger bowed to Krishna.

"I bring an urgent message from King Ugrasen, sire," the messenger said. "Shishupal's friend King Salwa has attacked Dwarika! The king has asked you to return speedily, milord."

"That coward!" Balram exploded on hearing the news. "He attacks when we are away!"

"He must be upset over Shishupal's death," Satyaki opined.

"Come on, ride your chariots," Krishna said with some urgency. "Let's head home."

They drove the horses hard. When they were still some distance from the coast, they saw smoke rise in the sky in the distance. That made them ride even faster. As they neared their beloved city, they saw the walls of the island city broken in many places. The war machines on the turrets were damaged. The bridges to the city were destroyed. They rode in slowly over the makeshift bridge in place at the main gate. As they rode along the main avenue, they saw several buildings on fire. Mass pyres were lit on the cremation ground for the soldiers who had laid down their life while defending their city. The delightful parks were destroyed with large pits in their midst. The roof of the magnificent assembly hall, of which the residents of Dwarika were so proud, had caved in. Krishna was excessively pained at the sight of destruction to his beloved city.

King Ugrasen solemnly greeted Krishna and Balram. Other Yadav leaders like Akrur and Krutavarma were present.

Also were present Krishna's sons, Pradyumn from Rukmini and Samba from Jambuwati. They all were clad in armour and sat on broken seats in the assembly hall.

"King Salwa chose to attack when you were not here," the old king began. "As you know he was very close to Shishupal. They had both participated on the attack on Mathura. When he came to know of Shishupal's demise at your hands in Indraprasth, he came from his capital in the north and encircled Dwarika.

"Salwa's land forces ravaged the Yadav towns and villages in the open land. His battleships were out in the sea outside the cliff of the island. We closed the gates of the city and sealed every entrance as we prepared for battle. Every able-bodied man was asked to join the force. The city was put on high alert and men were forbidden from drinking so they remained watchful as long as the city was under attack. We drove out travelling jugglers, mimes and dancers least they act as spies and informers. Spikes were placed in trenches around the fort. No one was allowed to enter or leave the fort without proper identification marks. Our fort is naturally strong and our city was prepared more than ever to meet the enemy."

"Those were appropriate measures," Krishna nodded his appreciation. "What happened next?"

"When Krutavarma and Akrur were preparing to lead the Yadav troops to battle, your sons Pradyumn and Samba offered to lead the attack. We were a bit concerned in sending the young men to face the formidable enemy. But they insisted."

"That is so becoming of you two," Krishna was proud of his sons. "What did the two do?"

"With support from our archers stationed high on towers, they led our chariots against Salwa," Krutavarma said. "I and Akrur were stationed on the watch tower. Looking at the array of enemy forces from our vantage point, we directed our forces. Samba attacked the left flank and Pradyumn headed the frontal attack. Soon Samba encountered Kshema, Salwa's commander and chief counsellor advancing with a black standard fluttering on his chariot. He let loose a volley of arrows towards Samba who countered it with arrows cutting down his shafts. When his shafts were rendered useless, Kshema resorted to illusion. He had learned the art of magical warfare from the Asur allies.

Luckily for us, Samba's grandfather Jambuwant, king of the bears, had taught Samba the art of combating illusion. When his efforts were rendered useless Kshema withdrew signalling to a demon commander to take his place. Even as the demonic fighter took his place, Samba rushed at him and hurled a huge mace at him. Struck with that mace the demon fell like a tree. With that the left flank of the enemy was broken."

"Pradyumn advancing in the centre, encountered fierce resistance," Akrur recounted. "We directed the cavalry to enforce him. Salwa advanced on his grand chariot. Beholding Salwa on that amazing car of his, the combatants of Dwarika wavered with fear. But Pradyumn sailed out, and bidding the Yadavs to be of good cheer, roared, "Waver you not, and staying behold me fight! Fear not! The enemy will be slain today!"

"Rukmini's son," Akrur continued, spread confusion among the warriors of the city of Salwa. No one could mark the slightest interval between his successive shafts. He rushed with speed against Salwa himself so desirous of an encounter. Braved by the heroic Pradyumn in that mighty battle, the angry Salwa could ill bear the challenge! And that conqueror of hostile cities, Salwa, maddened by anger, riding his beautiful car of unchecked speed, resolved to encounter Pradyumn. Both the armies beheld the fight between Salwa and the foremost of Vrishni heroes.

"The illustrious and mighty Salwa began to discharge his arrows at Pradyumn. Pradyumn also overwhelmed Salwa by a thick shower of arrows. Beholding King Salwa fallen down deprived of sense, his army started fleeing away. But regaining his senses, the mighty Salwa rose and all of a sudden discharged his arrows on Pradyumn. Pradyumn, whose attention had wavered just for a moment on seeing Salwa fall, was sorely pierced by his adversary about his throat. Pradyumn became motionless on the field of battle!

"Great joy was felt by the enemy and seeing Pradyumn deprived of sense, his trained charioteer carried him off the field in the car. The chariot had not gone far when Pradyumn regained his senses, and taking up his bow addressed his charioteer, saying, 'Oh, what have you done? This is not the custom of the Vrishni heroes in battle! Turn the car! Never again fly from the field as you have done! What will my father say to me when he hears that I have left the field of battle.'

The charioteer replied, 'You were much afflicted and wounded by the arrows shot by Salwa. You were also deprived of thy senses. Therefore I retired from the field. But, now that you have regained senses, witness my skill in guiding the horses!'"

Akrur continued, "Then Salwa again discharged at your son a shower of various kinds of weapons. But Pradyumn showing with a smile his lightness of hand, cut all those weapons off as they reached him. Pradyumn discharged winged shafts at the king. Salwa, thus afflicted by the Vrishnis, mounted on his car of precious metals, and leaving Dwarika scudded through the skies!"

"Oh, he withdrew?" Krishna asked. "Then how did all this destruction of the city take place?"

"His leaving the battlefield was a deception," King Ugrasen said with a sigh. "He had of late obtained a wonderful chariot from Lord Shiva. As you know Lord Shiva is so simple-minded, some might even call him naive! Time and again the Asurs and wicked minded people worship him and when he is pleased he grants them boons without considering the consequences. This Salwa also worshipped the trident-wielding Shiva and was granted this chariot as a boon. The chariot is made of precious metals and is capable of flying through the skies at great speed.

"No sooner had the Yadav forces returned to the city thinking that Salwa had retreated, his car loomed over the horizon. With a great speed he descended on the city and fired missiles. He hit the bridges and the war engines on the ramparts. He rained fireballs on our men killing hundreds, while we watched helplessly. He set buildings on fire, destroyed our assembly hall and went away whooping in glee in that aerial car."

"Oh, that conniving coward!" Krishna was thunderous at Salwa's manoeuvre. "I think he will keep on attacking Dwarika whenever the leaders are out of town. This matter must be settled once for all."

"Yes, indeed," Pradyumn rose from his seat with enthusiasm, "give us the order and we will put an end to him."

"I will deal with him myself," Krishna said. "However, I

do not want you all heroes to accompany me, for that sly Salwa might strike Dwarika again. Satyaki, Krutavarma, Pradyumn, and Samba you hold the fort while I go after that wicked, demonic king."

With a company of select warriors on horseback, Krishna left Dwarika in his chariot to which were yoked the best of steeds. His trusted charioteer Daruk handled the horses. They travelled for two days crossing many rivers, ravines and hills. While they were still far from Salwa's city, they met Yadav spies whom Krishna had sent ahead to gather whereabouts of Salwa. They informed Krishna that Salwa was not in his city but at a resort in an island off the west coast. Krishna changed the course and headed to the coast.

They travelled another day and reached the coast. While his warriors rested and prepared for battle Krishna scouted the land. From atop a hill abutting the shore, he spotted the island at some distance with Salwa's chariot gleaming in the morning sun.

Krishna, standing atop the hill, blew his pure white conch shell challenging Salwa to a battle. As the sound of the conch reached the island, Krishna saw Salwa and his chosen demonic guards stir. All of a sudden a change in the weather took place. A thick mist covered the island. The sun turned pale and darkness enveloped the land. Stars shone in the sky. Krishna realized that Salwa had resorted to demonic magic. He heard a whirr in the sky and realized Salwa's chariot was now airborne.

Krishna sat in his chariot and shut his eyes. Using his yogic powers he dispelled Salwa's magic. The sun shone again and he opened his eyes. He saw Salwa's car above him. Arrows flew from that aerial vehicle and covered the Yadav horsemen, leading to heavy casualties. Krishna shot arrows cutting down the shower of arrows from above.

When his arrows were rendered ineffective, Salwa resorted to magic again. The sky became full of dust clouds and hot ashes and embers started raining down on Krishna's army. Krishna deployed the rain weapon and washed away the dust clouds.

About this time a resident of Dwarika approached Krishna's carriage.

"King Ugrasen has sent me," he told Krishna in a voice choked with sorrow. "While fighting with you, Salwa's car momentarily appeared in the city and he slew your father Vasudev!" Krishna was aghast at the news.

"There is no need to continue the battle," the messenger continued, "the king has asked you to return to Dwarika and defend it."

His heart heavy at the news, Krishna was unable to decide whether to return to Dwarika or continue the battle. He was enraged at Akrur, Balram, Satyaki and Krutavarma for not protecting his father. While he was in such a state of mind, he saw his father Vasudev fall down from Salwa's vehicle high up in the sky. His headgear came loose and his hair flowed as he fell. The bow dropped from Krishna's hand and he swooned at that sight. He sat on the chariot. He heard Salwa's delirious laughter from his car in the sky. The messenger disappeared all of a sudden. That made Krishna realize that the news was false and it was an illusion created by Salwa. He got up and fixed an arrow on his bow with a mantra to dispel the illusion. The battle resumed and Salwa and Krishna started sending missiles at each other.

It was at this juncture that Krishna heard Draupadi's wail in his mind. "O, Krishna, you consider me your sister and I am in distress. Where are you? See how your sister is being dishonoured in the court of Hastinapur."

For a moment Krishna thought this was yet another illusion created by Salwa. However, he could not risk it being real. If Draupadi was really in trouble, he had to help her. He kept his weapon aside and concentrated his mind on Draupadi, his deemed sister and queen of the Pandavs. He created a shield of light around his chariot and leaving his body in the vehicle on the battlefield, his soul arrived in Hastinapur. He saw her in the court hall at Hastinapur. The blind King Dhrutarashtra was on his throne. Grandsire Bhishm and minister Vidur sat with their heads bowed in shame. He saw the Pandavs sitting on a rostrum with Duryodhan and his uncle Shakuni, the wicked prince of Gandhar. They seemed to be gambling with the dice. The Pandav brothers seemed humiliated, while Duryodhan and his aides seemed jubilant. As he watched, Duryodhan's younger brother, Duhshasan, advanced towards Draupadi. He caught the end of her garment and started tugging at it.

"O Krishna," Draupadi's piteous words rang in his ears. "Can't you see that the Kauravs are humiliating me? O destroyer of all afflictions rescue me, who am sinking in the ocean of grief. O Krishna, O Krishna, O you great yogi, save me who am distressed—who am losing my senses in the midst of the Kurus." Covering her face she cried aloud.

Hearing the words of Draupadi, Krishna was deeply moved. And remembering how she had torn her robe to make a bandage for him, remaining unseen, he covered her with excellent clothes of many hues. As the attire of Draupadi was being pulled by Duhshasan, after one was taken off, another of the same kind, appeared covering her. Hundreds upon hundreds of robes of many hues came off Draupadi's person, until her tormentor fell down exhausted. There arose a deep uproar of from the assembled kings in the Kuru court.

Having accomplished the deliverance of Draupadi from the calamity that had befallen her, Krishna brought his soul back to his body. He was eager to know what had befallen the Pandavs. Resolved to put an end to the conflict with the deceitful Salwa, he summoned his disc weapon and it whirred in his hand. He released the Sudarshan disc which circled once around Salwa's vehicle of strong metal and cleaved it into two along with Salwa in it. As the pieces of that magical car along with the body of Salwa fell down there was a great uproar in the sky and a flowery shower on Krishna from the celestials.

As soon as victorious Krishna reached Dwarika, even before the celebrations, he dispatched messengers on speedy steeds to Hastinapur to know of the happenings there. He did not have to wait long for a messenger arrived from Hastinapur's minister Vidur.

"A great calamity has befallen the Pandavs, milord," the messenger informed Krishna. "Having seen the great wealth of the Pandavs, a jealous Prince Duryodhan invited Emperor Yudhisthir to a match of dice at Hastinapur. Duryodhan's uncle, the treacherous Shakuni, who knows many tricks with the dice, cheated Yudhisthir. The emperor got carried away and lost his empire, his brothers, and his queen in subsequent wagers. Queen Draupadi was humiliated by Duryodhan's brother, but was miraculously saved from disrobement. In the last wager, King Yudhisthir accepted to a life of exile in the forest for twelve years, followed by an year of living in disguise. They have left the Kuru capital and are in the forest now."

"So this was no magical illusion of Salwa," Krishna said, "a real calamity has befallen dear Pandavs. Prepare my chariot, I shall visit them now in the forest."

15. The Empty Bowl

There was excitement in the hamlets and hermitages in the forest of Kamyak as word spread that Krishna had arrived to meet the Pandavs. Subhadra arrived from Indraprasth with her son Abhimanyu and Draupadi's five sons. Scores of citizens also arrived from Indraprasth. Draupadi's brother Dhrushtadyumna came from Kampilya.

"Krishna!" A lamenting Draupadi rushed to him as soon as she saw him, "you have arrived too late. All is over. I am a daughter-in-law of the Kurus yet I was humiliated in their court in front of all the elders. My mighty warrior husbands watched it all silently. You are my brother and protector, then how did this happen in the first place?" As she spoke, Draupadi's tears flowed freely.

"If I were around, I would have never let the game of dice take place. I would have prevailed upon Dhrutarashtra, Bhishm, teacher Krupa and guru Dron to stop the game of dice before it had taken such a course." Krishna was moved by Draupadi's plight. "Unfortunately I was tied down in warfare with Salwa at that time. I promise you my dear sister; those who have committed this heinous crime will not go unpunished."

"Let us gather our forces and attack Hastinapur and punish those evil Kauravs!" Dhrushtadyumna was enraged on hearing first-hand the account of his sister's humiliation at the Kuru court.

"Yes!" The Yadav heroes Satyaki and Krutavarma from Dwarika who had accompanied Krishna also supported him. "Let us attack Hastinapur and do away with the vile sons of Dhrutarashtra."

"This is no time for war," Yudhisthir said pacifying them, "I entered the game of dice of my own free will and I have to honour the terms. I must spend twelve years in the forest."

"He's right," Krishna said. The others had to back down at that. Krishna turned to Draupadi, "When we face calamities we wonder why they take place. When good times visit us, do we wonder why we have them? Good and bad times come in cycles, not only for humans but for the entire universe. Do not accept this misfortune as ultimate; it may be there for some purpose."

They fell silent as Krishna's words made them see the events in a different light.

"I will take Draupadi and her sons to Kampilya," Dhrushtadyumna broke the silence, "the forest is no place for these children to grow up."

"The children need not suffer. You take them to Kampilya with you. But I shall suffer the hardships of the forest life along with my husbands." Draupadi was firm on her resolve.

"Let Subhadra and Abhimanyu come with me to Dwarika," Krishna offered, "I shall attend to Abhimanyu's education."

Krishna and Satyabhama spent some days with the Pandavs. He spoke to them of the days to come and how they should be spent. Satyabhama and Subhadra spent time with Draupadi trying to lighten her grief by diverting her mind.

Draupadi was quite impressed by Satyabhama's personality. One day along with Subhadra and Satyabhama she retreated to a shady grove while the Pandavs entertained Krishna in the hut.

"She is imperious they say, but that suits her personality so well!" Draupadi thought as she admired Satyabhama's agile and athletic figure.

"Tell me Draupadi," Satyabhama said in an intimate tone after they had exchanged pleasantries, "Each of your life partners is a great warrior and hero in his own right, yet not one of them ever speaks a harsh word with you. How do you manage to rule the hearts of five husbands when most women find it so difficult to control one? Do you practice some incantation or drug at the time of the bath or some secret science, or the recitation of occult formulae, or maybe medicines?"

"Oh no, never!" Draupadi laughed. She had heard about the intense jealousy Satyabhama felt towards Rukmini, Krishna's first wife. Rukmini and Satyabhama were so different in temperament. Rukmini was quiet, pleasant to speak to and devoted to Krishna, who had rescued her from an unwanted marriage. Satyabhama was strong-willed, dominating and threw tantrums at the slightest provocation. A repentant Satyabhama's father had offered her hand to Krishna in marriage after he had wrongly accused Krishna of stealing his prized jewel.

"Women who resort to wicked methods like spells and drugs cannot retain the faith of their mates for long and ultimately lose them. You know the best drug or incantation is that of love and devotion." Draupadi said. Satyabhama appreciated how Draupadi had chosen to be with Yudhisthir even after he had lost her in an insane gambling match.

"In practical terms it means a lot of hard work, the Pandavs are warriors but very bad at bookkeeping. With hundreds of guests arriving every day, I had to take care of all of the in-house stocks and looked after the royal treasury of Indraprasth. Not that the ministers there were untrustworthy; in fact they were quite honest, but, it's better to let them know that someone is supervising, so circumstances do not tempt an honest person." Satyabhama had not known that Draupadi was behind the excellent management of Indraprasth.

"Even here in the wilderness," Draupadi continued, "I have so many dependents to take care of and guests to feed. Luckily we have the celestial bowl given by the sun god to Yudhisthir. It produces as much food as we want. However, once it is washed after a meal, it does not produce food for eight more hours."

"But don't you feel jealous that Arjun married Ulupi, Chitrangada..." Satyabhama said looking at Subhadra.

"No, I don't go on and on about some princess they might have met while on long campaigns, but I don't allow them to bring them back to my palace either."

"Except allowing Arjun to bring Subhadra..." Satyabhama's observation made them all laugh.

"Oh, Subhadra is such a sweet girl," Draupadi said. Then she lowered her tone, it was her turn now to know secrets. "Tell me Satyabhama, is it true what I hear?"

"Are you referring to Krishna's marrying thousands of women?" Obviously, Satyabhama did not believe in mincing words. "Yes, it's true."

"But, how...and why?"

"Well, because I helped him," Satyabhama laughed as Draupadi uttered a cry of disbelief.

"Tell me all, please." Draupadi was so curious now.

"This demon King Naraka from Pragjothishyapur had become too powerful for his own good," Satyabhama began. " I went with Krishna on the mission to defeat him and rescue the sixteen thousand women he had imprisoned. When Naraka was defeated, we had the problem of rehabilitating the rescued women. Krishna arranged for them to come to Dwarika. When we flew back on Garud, Krishna ordered dwellings built before their arrival at Dwarika. They are now the responsibility of the Yadav state. We proffer livelihood for those who prefer to stay.

"That's how I helped Krishna get his 'sixteen thousand wives'." Satyabhama finished with a smile.

"That was so wonderful of you and Krishna. And like a fool I thought..." Draupadi felt silly. She could not but admire the awesome warrior queen, born as she herself was from fire.

One day after lunch and after all the dependent families who had chosen to accompany King Yudhisthir in the forest were fed, Draupadi washed the sun pot. The women were looking forward to a long siesta in the cool breeze under the Neem tree near the cottage. After the Pandavs and Krishna retired to their huts for a nap, Draupadi was unfolding grass mats under the cool shade of her favourite tree when she heard a shout and looked up. Two little boys from the forest tribes came running.

"A large troop of sages is headed this way, milady," one of them exclaimed, panting from the exertion.

"We saw them across the river," the other one added. The commotion brought the Pandavs out of their huts.

"I will go and see who it is," Sahdev went with the boys. Presently one of the boys returned at the double.

"Prince Sahdev says it's the Sage Durvas, who has come all the way from Hastinapur," he reported between gasps, "and the sage has asked to keep meals ready for his followers. Tired and dusty from the journey, they are taking a bath at the river. They will soon be here."

"Yes, of course, we have to arrange for the lunch of our

revered guests," Yudhisthir said as he hurried towards the river to receive the Sage.

"Oh, no! Not Sage Durvas!" Bheem groaned. "What have we done to deserve his visit?"

Krishna smiled. Bheem had reason enough to despair. Durvas was a peculiar sage. While he was revered all over the land for his knowledge of scriptures and his ascetic power, people were scared of him for he had a curse or two always ready on the tip of his tongue. He had the dubious reputation of cursing people right and left if they happened to displease him in the slightest manner.

"I am sure that wicked Duryodhan must have sent him here from Hastinapur," Arjun said. "If we fail to please the sage, he will lay some curse on us and add to our misery!"

"What shall I do now?" Draupadi was quite upset by the unexpected arrival of the guests, "I have washed the Sun bowl already." She went to the kitchen hut to look, though she knew there wasn't a morsel left.

Bheem and Arjun looked at each other. They knew about the short temper of the sage. Not knowing what more they could do, they followed their elder brother to the river. Some of the women from among the *Brahmins* and the tribes from the forest came to help Draupadi.

"I shall fetch some fruits," one of them suggested.

"Let's light the fire and cook some rice," Satyabhama offered.

They started discussing what and how to cook. Draupadi did not discourage those kind souls, but she knew this was not going to help. Time was too short to cook for a hundred sages. *'As if we did not have enough grief on our plate already,'* she thought. *'What shall I do now?'* Feeling helpless, she stood looking at the women frantically trying to help her.

"I am so hungry, my sister," she heard Krishna's voice and turned towards the door. Krishna stood smiling there. "Give me something to eat now."

"Oh, Krishna!" she exclaimed, "I am already worried about feeding the hundred odd sages and now you!"

"Forget the sages," Krishna brushed past her into the kitchen, looking into the empty pots, "all I can think of now is a bite for myself." He spotted the sparkling clean Sun bowl resting upturned.

"I washed it only moments before they arrived, Krishna," Draupadi lamented. "Why is fate playing cruel games with me?"

"Let me see the bowl," Krishna ignored her words, "may be there's something left at the bottom."

"No chance," Draupadi fetched the bowl and handed over to him. He turned it over watching closely. He saw a tiny shred of a vegetable at one edge.

"Ah," he smiled happily, "this will suffice."

He picked it on the tip of his finger and placed it on his tongue. Draupadi looked at him in astonishment as he belched happily.

"Now that I have eaten," he said, "tell me what's bothering you."

"The guests, Krishna!" Draupadi said in exasperation, "they will be here any moment expecting a meal. And you know well what Sage Durvas can do if he is displeased."

"I have a feeling they won't be coming for lunch," Krishna was nonchalant. Smiling at Draupadi, he went outside, took out the flute tucked in his waistband and sat cross-legged under the Neem tree playing it.

When Yudhisthir arrived near the river, he saw a group of sages on the far bank, but there was something odd going on. They seemed to be leaving, their water pots swaying in their hands as they hurried up the slope of the river bank.

"What happened, Sahdev?" he asked his brother who stood there, also surprised.

"I can't understand this," Sahdev looked baffled. "I overheard them saying to each other, 'I am not hungry anymore; I feel as if I had full meal already.' And Sage Durvas said, 'How can we show ourselves at Yudhisthir's place now? It's too awkward a situation. After we ask them to cook, we can't eat! We better leave before he arrives to receive us.' They donned their deerskins in a hurry and are leaving now."

"Strange, indeed!" Yudhisthir shook his head.

On their way back to camp, they met Bheem, Arjun and Nakul. They stopped in the middle of the footpath discussing what could have made the sages abruptly change their mind.

"Listen!" Arjun cocked his head, "I hear Krishna's flute."

"Now I understand," Yudhisthir smiled. "It's Krishna's doing."

The Pandavs rushed back to the cottages and saw Krishna smiling. The cousins embraced him happily.

"You must have chased the sages away!" Arjun said.

"My sister needed my help," Krishna smiled at Draupadi.

After a short, pleasant stay of a few days with the Pandavs in the forest he left for Dwarika with Satyabhama, Subhadra and Abhimanyu.

16. The Mediator

"The Pandavs have appeared in King Virat's court!"

There was excitement among the Yadavs when the messenger from Yudhisthir arrived at Dwarika to the effect that the Pandavs had fulfilled the terms of the dice game. They had spent twelve years in the forest and one year of living incognito. They had spent the last year in King Virat's land living in disguise as servants to the king and queen.

Krishna along with Balram, Satyaki and Krutavarma immediately left for Virat's country. The guests rested that night and presented themselves in King Virat's court next morning. The seats in the court were arranged according to protocol for the distinguished royals attending the conference of Pandav's friends.

King Virat invited King Drupad, Draupadi's father, to grace a throne placed next to his. On one side of those kings, sat Yudhisthir and his four brothers; and seats on the other side were taken by Krishna, Balram, the Panchal warriors Dhrushtadyumna and Shikhandi, and the Yadavs Satyaki and Krutavarma.

"Now that the one and twelve years, as laid down in the terms of the game of dice, are over," King Virat began, "The next course of action must be decided."

"It is for us to consider what will be for the good of both Kauravs and the Pandavs, what will be consistent with righteousness, and what will meet with the approbation of all," Krishna said. "When we do not know what the other side thinks, what opinion can we form? Therefore, let an able ambassador be sent to beseech the Kauravs to give half the kingdom to Yudhisthir."

"Indeed, an excellent suggestion." Having listened to Krishna's pacific speech of impartial spirit, Balram lauded his younger brother and added, "Yudhisthir, though a worthy and just king, lost his kingdom due to his addiction to gambling.

The ambassador we send should implore King Dhrutarashtra and Duryodhan to accede—"

"Excuse me." Satyaki, the Yadav general, was on his feet even as Balram was speaking. "The whole world knows that Yudhisthir conceded to the game of dice because he thinks it is the duty of a *Kshatriya* to respond to a challenge and the vile Shakuni cheated. Moreover, is Yudhisthir a panhandler that his ambassador should supplicate to that wretched regent king of Hastinapur? He is asking for his own land. To be a beggar before foes is impious. Our ambassador should convey a strong message—'Give Yudhisthir his due, or else.'"

"Sending ambassadors is a waste of time where Duryodhan and his blind father are concerned," King Drupad said. "Never will Duryodhan give up the kingdom by peaceful means, and Dhrutarashtra, who dotes on his son, will follow him in his wish."

"Not words but arrows should carry our message to Hastinapur." Dhrushtadyumna opined.

"I will blast away the Kauravs from the face of earth for the insult they offered to Draupadi!" Bheem thundered.

"Let us march on Hastinapur now!" Satyaki sounded off.

"I have intelligence that Duryodhan is already contacting kingdoms across Aryavart for support," King Drupad said. "Having access to the treasuries of both Hastinapur and Indraprasth, he has appeased many a king and gained their allegiance. Let us also prepare ourselves. Let us send word to our friends that they may collect an army for us. Let speedy messengers go to Shalya, and Ketu, and Yatsena, and the prince of the Kekayas."

They all looked at Krishna, who was watching their reactions.

"We are not talking of a skirmish or even a battle here, gentlemen. This war, if it takes place, will engulf entire Aryavart. It will be a terrible war covering the earth in a mire of flesh and blood. War can be justified only as the *ultimate* means towards a just end. All other avenues should be explored before one can think of war," Krishna began and Yudhisthir nodded his assent. Krishna's stern tone sobered others to some extent. He strode up and down the aisle as he declared with finality, "First of all, send an envoy to Hastinapur and attempt peaceful resolution. Meanwhile, lest you are taken unawares, let Yudhisthir's emissaries go to all amiable kings, just in case."

King Virat suggested his chief priest, an elderly and intelligent person, for the mission to Hastinapur. When the meeting ended, Krishna returned to Dwarika along with Balram and other Yadav heroes. The Pandavs moved to Upaplavya, a quiet town northeast of Virat's bustling capital closer to Hastinapur, and set camp there.

One afternoon as Krishna rested after lunch in his palace, he felt someone's presence near him. He opened his eyes and saw Arjun standing at the foot of his lounge.

"Arjun!" he exclaimed. He became aware of someone sitting near his head and turned to see Duryodhan seated there. "...And Duryodhan too. What a pleasant surprise. Have you both reached a compromise already?"

"Actually I came to seek your support, in the war," Duryodhan said quickly, before Arjun could speak.

"And you Arjun?" Krishna asked.

"I came seeking your help too," Arjun replied.

"But I arrived here first!" Duryodhan exclaimed.

"I see," Krishna said. "But I saw Arjun first."

Duryodhan's heart sank. *He favours Arjun,* he thought. They both waited anxiously as Krishna thought for a moment.

"Duryodhan came here first and I saw Arjun first, so I cannot deny either of you. I offer you an option: you can choose my army with elephants, camels, chariots, cavalry, infantry and all the equipment or you can choose me. And be warned, I shall not bear arms in this conflict, if at all it takes place," he said.

Krishna watched both Duryodhan and Arjun brighten at his proposal.

"Arjun is younger than you, Duryodhan," Krishna said, "so let him have the first choice."

"I choose you, Krishna." Arjun did not have to think at all.

"I get your entire army!" Duryodhan exclaimed, unable to contain his glee.

Krishna had managed to give them both what they wanted. Duryodhan thanked Krishna profusely, took his leave, and went to meet the elder brother Balram.

"Why did you choose me over my army, when I am not

even going to wield a weapon?" Krishna asked.

"I don't need another army, Krishna. Between me and Bheem we can take on the Kauravs," Arjun said. "What we need is an adviser, and who is greater in wisdom than you on earth? Will you be my charioteer, so I can stay close to you through the battles?"

"Why, of course, if there is a war!" Krishna laughed.

"What have you done, Krishna?" Satyaki, with Krutavarma in his tow, rushed in Krishna's chamber when Duryodhan left. "Duryodhan says, you offered the whole army to the Kauravs! But there's no way I am going to fight against the Pandavs."

"It's for you to choose," Krishna said with a smile. "I won't insist on anyone to choose sides."

"I will fight for the Pandavs." Satyaki seemed relieved.

"As for me, I go where the army goes," Krutavarma said. "But I will remain with you until war is declared."

Just then Balram entered Krishna's chamber. "Duryodhan wanted me to fight for the Kauravs. But I don't want to be a party to this fratricidal war," he said, "I am not going to fight for either the Pandavs or Kauravs."

"If there is a war..." Krishna replied with a smile. "We are negotiating for peace, remember?"

"You know my position if war takes place," Balram said and left.

"I want to be present when Dhrutarashtra's ambassador arrives from Hastinapur," Krishna said, when Arjun told him about the message Dhrutarashtra had sent with King Virat's priest. Krishna, Satyaki, and Krutavarma left for Upaplavya with Arjun. They had barely joined Yudhisthir and others under the big top in the centre of the encampment, when Virat's guards announced the arrival of King Dhrutarashtra' charioteer Sanjay.

"The King has not chosen to send Uncle Vidur this time," Yudhisthir observed. "These days he prefers the soft-spoken Sanjay to the straightforward minister for advice."

On a signal from King Virat, the guards escorted Sanjay to the tent. He bowed to the royals present at the Pandav council. After they had exchanged pleasantries, Yudhisthir asked him, "What message has my uncle sent with you, Sanjay?"

"My King expresses great delight that you have come

back from the forest safe. He also appreciates your virtuous behaviour, my lord," Sanjay said. "He is confident that you possess the esoteric principles and know how short-lived are the pleasures that material possessions bring, while the long-lasting ones are of the spiritual plane. Material desires are never-ending and lead to more desires. He hopes you will not take the path of war for such momentary material gains.

"You and your brothers are well-versed in the science of weapons and have guidance of the venerable Krishna, and are assisted by Satyaki and Dhrushtadyumna and Shikhandi. Even the lord of celestials cannot defeat you. Similarly, on the Kaurav side is Grandsire Bhishm; Gurus Dron and Krupa; Karn, the King of Ang; Prince Duryodhan and the preceptor's son Ashwatthama, are all towering champions in their own right. Who, without loss to himself, is able to slay the vast force assembled by Dhrutarashtra's son? Therefore, I do not see any good either in victory or in defeat for either side. By defeating and slaying all your foes, will the subsequent life of yours not be equivalent to death, for, in truth, what is life after having killed all your kinsfolk?"

"Why does our uncle talk of war, Sanjay?" Yudhisthir asked. "All I am asking is that the legitimate portion of the kingdom be given to us."

"If without war, Duryodhan will not yield your share of the kingdom, King Dhrutarashtra thinks, it is far better for you to live seeking alms in the kingdom of the Yadavs, the Panchals, and the Matsyas than obtain sovereignty by war," Sanjay said. "You have done mighty deeds that will be good for you in the higher world to come, and they are admired by righteous men. There, in the next world on the celestial plane, one is free from death, decrepitude, fear, hunger, and thirst, and from all that is disagreeable to the mind. Therefore, do not any longer desire this earthly kingdom."

"King Dhrutarashtra makes vice assume the aspects of virtue and virtue itself seem as vice," Yudhisthir replied. "Desirous of satisfying his sons, he knowingly enters upon an unrighteous course. Indeed, on account of his fondness for his son, he does not pay heed to Vidur, who, out of all the Kauravs, is the wisest and best of all his well-wishers, possessing vast learning, and righteous in act. That son, who seeks honours from others, but is himself envious and wrathful, whose tongue is foul, whose soul is absorbed in sensual pleasures, and who, full of unfriendly feelings to many, obeys no law, and whose life is evil, heart implacable, and understanding vicious—for such a son King Dhrutarashtra knowingly abandoned the path of virtue. Now he discourses on the path of alms for us to follow. Let Krishna, who is impartial to both and seeks the welfare of both sides, say what the right course is for us."

"I desire," Krishna said, "that the sons of Pandu should not be ruined; that they may prosper, and attain their wishes. Similarly, I pray for the prosperity of King Dhrutarashtra and his sons. Peace is desirable both for the Kauravs and the Pandavs. Yudhisthir has displayed a peaceful disposition of a very rare character. However, when Dhrutarashtra and his sons are so covetous—why should hostility not run high? King Dhrutarashtra cannot pretend to be more versed than I or Yudhisthir, in the principles of right and wrong. Why should anyone speak words of reproach about Yudhisthir who from the very beginning, in keeping with treatises of morality, has thought of the welfare of the entire Kuru clan? You advise Yudhisthir to give up the earthly kingdom in preference to the celestial one. I know there are learned men who advocate renunciation and retreat, but I am not for giving up one's duty in worldly matters. One can attain the highest spiritual plane by sedulously performing one's duty in this world. Supplicating to blatant injustice is not the duty of a head of a family and kingdom.

"I desire to go in person to the Kurus, in order to settle this matter. If without injury to the Pandavs' cause I succeed in bringing about peace, I will be extricating the Kauravs also from the mesh of death. The Kuru dynasty is like a great forest—the Kauravs are the trees and the Pandavs are tigers. The trees shelter the tigers and they in turn protect the trees. Let the King not drive the tigers away; the tigers out of the forest are easily slain and the trees are easily cut down if there are no tigers to protect them.

"I hope that when I speak words of wisdom to the Kauravs, Duryodhan will pay heed to them. Else you may rest assured that those vicious sons of Dhrutarashtra will be scorched by Arjun and Bheem in battle."

Sanjay took leave of Yudhisthir and left for Hastinapur to convey Krishna's intention of meeting the Kauravs for negotiations.

Draupadi came to know of Krishna's decision to mediate for peace.

"You seek peace with the Kauravs, Krishna? Have you forgotten how I was insulted in the Kuru court? Will there be no justice for me? Will my hair remain un-braided for the remainder of my life?" A furious Draupadi confronted Krishna, tossing about her loose hair.

"War should be treated with utmost gravity, Draupadi. In particular, this war, if it takes place, will see a million *Kshatriya* women widowed. And I mean to try my best to avoid it," he said in all solemnity. "I managed to mete out justice to Jarasandh without waging a war; however, with Narakasur I had no choice but to wage a war. So rest assured Draupadi, war or no war—your culprits will be chastened."

When Krishna started on his peace mission to Hastinapur in the morning, Yudhisthir, concerned over his safety, said, "One can't say what our wretched cousin will come up with next, Krishna."

"Don't worry, Yudhisthir," Krishna merely smiled as whirring in his hand in all its glory, the Sudarshan disc flashed for a moment and disappeared. Yudhisthir's anxiety was somewhat assuaged at the sight of that celestial weapon.

"I will go with Krishna," Satyaki announced. To Krutavarma, he said, "You have promised to remain with us until the war is announced."

"Of course, I am coming with you," Krutavarma said. "I have already ordered eight chariots of the best Yadav warriors to escort Krishna."

The Pandavs, the Virats and the Drupads followed Krishna for some distance along the way to the Elephant City. The populace living along the roads that Krishna's caravan passed witnessed wonderful omens. A delicious breeze blew and the atmosphere became auspicious. Wells and water-vessels overflowed. Lotuses and fragrant flowers bloomed everywhere. The very road became delightful, being free from prickly grass and thorns. Men, women, and children were all excited. They gathered in villages along the road where he camped at night and offered him vessels full of curds and butter and honey.

King Dhrutarashtra ordered pavilions and arches erected on the roads and the roads sprinkled with scented water. He planned to present Krishna sixteen chariots made of gold, each drawn by four steeds of the Vahlika breed. Also he thought of presenting him with eight elephants with tusks as large as poles of ploughs, capable of smiting hostile ranks, and each having eight of the best *mahout* attendants. He desired to give him eight hundred woollen blankets woven by the hill-men and also give him a thousand deerskins brought from China and the serene gem of the purest rays.

When Krishna arrived at the Kuru capital next morning he ignored all the arrangements made by the Kauravs to welcome him, but he gracefully accepted the spontaneous welcome afforded by the citizens and went to see Dhrutarashtra in the imperial apartments.

"You must be tired after the long journey," Dhrutarashtra said after pleasantries were exchanged and enquiries were made about the well-being of each other's clans, "Pray rest in Dussan's palace and we can meet tomorrow in the court after you are refreshed."

"I prefer Vidur's home, your majesty," Krishna declined, "but first I wish to see my aunt Kunti."

"Won't you have a bite at the luncheon we have hosted in your honour?" Duryodhan asked, trying to suppress his irritation.

"Envoys eat with hosts only after the success of their missions. Therefore, after my mission becomes successful, Prince of Hastinapur, you may entertain me and my attendants," Krishna said to Duryodhan's chagrin.

Born of a maid, Vidur led an austere life in a modest dwelling outside the palace precincts. Kunti had chosen to live in a part of Vidur's house instead of the palace, after the Pandavs had left for the forest. Her tears flowed freely when Krishna touched her feet. Kunti sniffed the head of her dear nephew and enquired after her sons and grandchildren.

"Will there be a war, Krishna?" she asked.

"I do not know yet," Krishna replied. "It depends on what Duryodhan chooses."

"How long am I to live on Vidur's charity?" Kunti said. "As a young girl, my father gave me away to his friend for adoption as one gives away a cow. I spent my girlhood in isolation in my foster father's palace and committed a blunder for which I am repenting even today. Out of adolescent excitement and girlish curiosity, I tried the mantra imparted by Sage Odoras and summoned the Sun. The son I bore and abandoned in my maidenhood was found by a charioteer and has turned into an avowed enemy of my other sons after being befriended by Duryodhan."

Krishna listened as Kunti poured her heart out.

"Soon after my marriage to King Pandu, he incurred the curse of the deer and we went to live in the forest. The years of happiness in bringing up the children I bore for him also ended when he died. Then I lived in Hastinapur as a widow, always in fear of what harm that wretched Duryodhan would inflict on my sons. The only time I lived an honourable life was in Indraprasth when Yudhisthir was emperor. He lost his empire in the game of dice and here I am now living on Vidur's kindness, while my sons live on Virat's largesse." Her words tugged at Krishna's heartstrings. He sensed she had something more to say and waited patiently. When Kunti spoke again there was steel in her words.

"Tell Yudhisthir, a *Kshatriya* mother does not bring forth sons to live on charity in her old age. Ask Yudhisthir to claim what is legitimately his and not capitulate to those who usurped his rights. It is better for a *Kshatriya* to blaze for a moment than live a life of humiliation."

"I will do whatever I can," Krishna promised.

That night Krishna and Vidur relaxed on the terrace under the starlit autumn sky.

"I do not know if your mission will be fruitful, Krishna," Vidur said. "It does not seem proper to me, that you should go into the midst of these wicked-minded wretches assembled together, Krishna."

"I know well the wickedness of Dhrutarashtra' son and the hostility of the *Kshatriyas* that have sided with him, Vidur,"

Krishna replied. "I have still come to the Kurus in the hope of liberating from the meshes of death the whole *Kshatriya* race. I will endeavour to bring about peace between the Pandavs and the Kauravs who are about to be slaughtered in battle. If Duryodhan judges me wrongly, I shall have the satisfaction of my own conscience. I have come here so the world may not afterwards say, 'though competent, still Krishna did not attempt to restrain the angry Kauravs and Pandavs from slaughtering one another.' It is to serve both the parties that I have come here. If the Kauravs choose not to heed my advice, it will, indeed, be a sad day for Aryavart."

"I really hope they will listen to you tomorrow and war will be averted." Vidur said. "I fear for both the Kauravs and Pandavs."

"You are quite right Vidur, as always. But isn't it better to cross the bridge when one gets there?" Krishna prepared to retire for the night. "Let's rest now; we have a long day ahead of us tomorrow."

Vidur was amazed to see how quickly Krishna fell asleep. *He fulfils his duties with total dedication and diligence, and does not overtly worry about the outcome,* Vidur thought with admiration.

At dawn a band of choristers and bards, gifted with melodious voices, awoke Krishna with their sweet songs. Krishna donned a silk garment of pale cream, which set his dark skin off. He wore his diadem adorned with the peacock feather and wore a rare gem in a gold chain around his neck. Looking at that exceptional jewel, Vidur smiled remembering Dhrutarashtra' ridiculous idea of bribing this man.

Duryodhan and Shakuni came to Vidur's home. Krishna greeted them both with sweet and courteous enquiries.

"King Dhrutarashtra is seated in his court, with all the Kurus headed by Bhishm and with all the kings of the land. They are all soliciting your presence," Shakuni said.

Krishna called for his charioteer Daruk, who having groomed the excellent steeds and polished the chariot until it shone, was all ready to go. Vidur followed Krishna in his own chariot. Duryodhan and Shakuni rode in the following chariot. Krishna's Yadav braves led by Satyaki and Krutavarma rode in chariots and elephants behind them. As the cavalcade entered the broad street leading to the palace, cymbals began to play, conchs began to be blown, and tabors were beaten. A thousand soldiers, attired in ceremonial uniforms, bearing swords and lances and axes, marched ahead followed by troupes of young boys and girls performing in front of Krishna's chariot. A full five hundred elephants and chariots followed that unvanquished hero of Yadav's race while he proceeded. All the citizens of the capital, men and women desirous of beholding Krishna, came out into the streets, and the terraces and balconies of the mansion were thronged by royal ladies. Stopping to accept garlands, listening to sweet speeches and returning the greetings as each deserved, Krishna went along the path, casting his eyes on all. At last, when he reached the Kuru court, his attendants from Dwarika blew their trumpets and filled the welkin with that blare. That whole assembly of kings trembled with delight on setting their eyes on Krishna.

The entire royal court of Hastinapur, with the kings and sages assembled there, stood up as Krishna entered flanked by Vidur and Satyaki. Krishna greeted the royals each according to his age and accepted the seat offered on the left side of King Dhrutarashtra. Duryodhan took a seat opposite him on the other side of the king.

After all the kings were seated and perfect silence had ensued, Krishna addressed Dhrutarashtra in his deep voice while everyone listened to him with rapt attention.

"In order that peace may be established between the Kauravs and the Pandavs without a slaughter of the heroes, I have come. I have no other business here. If, O King, you are willing, you may be able to allay that danger even yet. For peace, I think, is not difficult of acquisition. The establishment of peace depends on you and me. Set right your sons and I will set the Pandavs right. It will be to your profit, as also to the benefit of the Pandavs. Let those sons of Pandu be your allies. Supported by the Pandavs, you can attain both morality and profit. Together with the Pandavs, your kingdom will be invincible. Protected on all sides by sons, grandsons, fathers, brothers, and friends, you will be able to live in happiness.

"I see nothing but a great destruction in battle. Both sides are brave and skilled in weapons. Save them from the terrible danger that threatens them. Inflamed with wrath they will exterminate the population of earth. Save, O king, these monarchs, from the terrible danger that threatens them. Abandoning wrath and enmity, let these kings, embracing one another in peace, eating and drinking with one another, dressed in excellent robes and decked with garlands, and doing courtesies to one another, return to their respective homes.

"Let the affection you had for the Pandavs be revived in your bosom and let it lead to the establishment of peace. Deprived of their father while they were infants, you brought them up. Cherish them again now as if they were your own sons. It is your duty to protect them and especially it is so when they are distressed. At your command, they have suffered great misery most patiently. Now give them their right. The Pandavs, with their eyes turned towards righteousness, are maintaining a calm attitude, and what they have said is consistent with truth, virtue, and justice.

"Let the monarchs present here say," Krishna concluded his speech extending his hand towards those present in the court, "if my appeal is in keeping with truth and propriety or not."

All the rulers present applauded these words of Krishna within their hearts, but none of them ventured to say anything in the presence of Duryodhan. However, the Sages Narad, Parshum, and Kanva stood up one by one and made speeches in support of Krishna's proposal.

"O holy ones," The blind king spoke at last, "it is even so as Krishna and you all say. It is consistent with virtue and fraught with reason. My wish is precisely such. Nevertheless, I have no power to carry it out. You must persuade Duryodhan. Vidur, Bhishm, and even Gandhari have tried to convince him and failed."

"You have the strength to make peace, but not the will," Krishna told Dhrutarashtra.

"It behoves you, Krishna, to speak after considering all sides," Duryodhan spoke with some feeling. "Everybody is bent on finding fault with me alone. However, even after reflecting gravely, I do not find the least fault in me. In the game at dice that they had accepted with free will, the Pandavs were vanquished and we won their kingdom. What blame can be mine as regards that? Moreover, they were exposed before the year of living incognito was complete. Why do the Pandavs yet seek a quarrel with us, as if they were strong? What have we done to them? We shall not bow down to them in fear."

"The Pandavs did complete their term of living in disguise on the seventh day of the dark fortnight last month. There can be no dispute on that," Dron said.

"You think you have committed no offence against the Pandavs?" Bhishm roared unable to listen to Duryodhan's conceited speech. "As yet the Pandavs are not accoutered in mail, as yet Arjun's Gandiv rests inactive, as yet Yudhisthir, having modesty for his ornament, does not cast angry glances on your troops, so let hostility cease. As yet that mighty Bheem does not, mace in hand, grind hostile divisions, let peace be made with the Pandavs. As yet Nakul, Sahdev, Dhrushtadyumna, Virat, and Shikhandi all well-versed in arms, do not penetrate your ranks, and pour their arrowy showers. So let hostility cease.

"Let that emperor Yudhisthir the Just receive you with an embrace. Let the tidings of a cordial union be proclaimed in the cities of all the kings. Let the Earth be ruled by feelings of affection and let your heart be freed from the fever of jealousy and wrath."

As Duryodhan remained impassive, Dhrutarashtra sent for Gandhari, "Let his mother make him see sense." When she arrived, Gandhari spoke at length in all earnestness to Duryodhan urging him to give up the idea of a conflict and allow peace, but he was unmoved.

"Let me set forth a proposal for you to consider, so that an honourable settlement can be attained," Krishna made a last attempt at a breakthrough. "Yudhisthir does not insist on half the kingdom; give him only the city of Indraprasth, which he has built from a ruin."

"No way!" Duryodhan rejected the proposal outright.

"All right, let me make the last offer," Krishna said, "give the Pandavs five small villages on the border of your kingdom and you will not hear from them again."

"I shall not grant them even that much of land which may be covered by the point of a sharp needle," Duryodhan shouted. "I will lay myself down on the field of battle on a bed of arrows but never give in to the demands of Pandavs."

"You wish for the bed of heroes? Verily you shall have it," Krishna said as he rose to his feet. "Since you disregard words of wisdom, you, along with your counselors will surely lie down on the earth turned as morsels of dogs and jackals."

"You dare threaten me in my own court?" Duryodhan screamed as Krishna started walking down the aisle. "Arrest this impudent cowherd!"

"Krutavarma!" Satyaki called out to Krishna's escort party, but Krishna restrained his men with a signal and turned towards the throne. A change came over Krishna. Enveloped in a golden aura, he rose in stature as the assembly watched in awe. That effulgent figure had very different effects on different beholders: it delighted the hearts of many like Vidur and Bhishm and struck fear in the hearts of those like Duryodhan and Duhshasana. Weapons slipped from the trembling hands of the Kaurav guards, as they were stricken with dread. The vision lasted but for a moment and a smiling Krishna walked away from the Kaurav court.

As he proceeded to Vidur's home, he whispered an instruction to Satyaki. Later that afternoon, Krishna, having taken leave of Kunti, Vidur, Bhishm, and Dron, mounted his chariot and left Hastinapur.

At camp Upaplavya several kings had arrived. Since the ground at Upaplavya was not enough to accommodate their armies, Yudhisthir had directed them to the vast plains of Kurukshetra lying west of Hastinapur. Advance parties had already scouted that land for level ground abounding with grass, water, and firewood. Avoiding cemeteries, temples and asylums of sages, they erected camps.

The war council met after Krishna's return from Hastinapur.

"Duryodhan is a sprawling tree of evil passions, Karn is its trunk, Shakuni the branches, Duhshasana forms its abundant blossoms, and Dhrutarashtra is the root," Krishna said. "Those wicked wights did not accept what everyone else saw as reasonable and beneficial. On my proposal for granting five small villages in a corner of the kingdom, Duryodhan declined to part with even that much of land that the point of a needle can cover! When my attempt at conciliation failed, I even tried to sow dissent among Duryodhan's followers. I must say my attempts failed. It is now up to you to take a final decision." In keeping with the promise he had made to Karn, Krishna did not specify that he had tried to win over Karn.

"The Kauravs have left us with no options, really. We have to win back the kingdom of Indraprasth we had built," Yudhisthir said.

"The present month between monsoon and winter is a delightful one. Food, drink, and fuel are abundant now," Krishna said. "All plants and herbs are vigorous, all trees full of fruits, and there are no flies. The roads are free from mire, and the waters are of agreeable taste. The weather is neither very hot nor very cold. Seven days after, will be the day of the new moon. Let the battle commence then, for that day is presided over by Indra."

"Let our troops proceed to Kurukshetra," Yudhisthir ordered. "Let preparations for the war begin!" The war council received Yudhisthir's words with enthusiastic shouts of approval.

"Onward to the battlefield!" Bheem roared and the Pandav troops took up the cry, as they marched towards Kurukshetra.

On the southwest borders of that great prairie land, dotted with lakes and traversed by the rivers, the Pandavs built up tent cities to house their seven divisions consisting of warriors in excess of a hundred thousand as well as messengers, scribes, bards, priests, surgeons, mechanics, cooks, dancers, ladies of the night, spies, traders, and vendors. They erected stables near waterholes to house their innumerable beasts of war. They built stores in different parts of Kurukshetra to stock food and drink; weapons and spare parts and consumables for weapons; water and fodder for the animals.

The Kaurav forces, almost one and a half times larger than that of the Pandavs, occupied the eastern part of the vast plains leaving vast flat spaces in between for manoeuvres and battles. The Kauravs built a wide and flat road from Hastinapur to Kurukshetra so that their troops could access the supplies quickly.

On the night before the war began Krishna noticed that Yudhisthir was in a pensive mood.

"So much bloodshed, so much destruction for one

kingdom," Yudhisthir asked, "Is it worth when all the land and all the women and all the wealth on this Earth cannot satisfy the unchecked desires of even one person?"

"Remember our mother's message. It is better for a *Kshatriya* to blaze for a moment than live a life of humiliation." The four Pandav brothers, with Krishna's support, dissuaded Yudhisthir from withdrawing from the war.

"I made every attempt to avert this war," Krishna said, "but now that it is inevitable I will, by all means, see that you shall win it."

17. A Mother's Maledictions

An eerie silence greeted the messenger as he entered Hastinapur. A pall of dust hung over the skyline of the capital. Sage Vyas and Minister Vidur were with Dhrutarashtra. The blind regent with his blindfolded queen waited for Sanjay, the messenger, to speak.*

"All our forces have been destroyed, milord, in the eighteen days of war at Kurukshetra," Sanjay said without preamble. "All the Sam Saptaks, together with Easterners, the Southerners, the Northerners, and also the Westerners have all been slain. The kings that came from diverse realms have all gone to the regions of the dead. After Bhishm, Dron, Karn and Shakuni, your sons headed by Duryodhan have all laid down their lives."

"Why am I still alive, after hearing the news?" Dhrutarashtra drew a long breath.

"Through your own faults you have fallen into such distress. Vidur, Bhishm, and Krishna had offered counsels for your good. Why do you feel pain now, having rejected those counsels?" Sanjay asked. "The man who shrouds a burning coal within the folds of his sleeve and is burnt by the fire that is kindled by it, would be pronounced a fool if he grieves for his injuries."

Dhrutarashtra, tall and powerfully built though he was, fell down senseless on the ground. Vidur and the king's attendants sprinkled cool water over his face, and fanned him with palm leaves. Recovering his senses, Dhrutarashtra wept for a long while. "I shall put an end to my life," he said.

"Do not give way to despair, milord," Vidur said in an attempt to pacify his elder brother. "The learned say that the bodies of men are like clothes; in the course of time these are destroyed. The being within, however, is eternal. As a person,

---

*For description of the war, see the prequel to this book *Adventures of the Pandav Princes.*

casting off one attire, wears another, even such is the case with the bodies of all embodied beings. Creatures obtain weal or woe as the fruit of their own acts. Through their acts, they obtain heaven, bliss, or hell. Whether able or unable, they have to bear their burdens which are the result of their own acts."

"This destruction of the Kurus was inevitable," Vyas spoke after Vidur. "Decades ago, I had travelled to Svarg. There, I beheld all the denizens of heaven in the celestial assembly. That day, the Earth in her embodied form, had repaired to the gods on a particular mission. Approaching the chief of gods in Svarg, she said, 'The sins of men have become unbearable. Rid me of that burden.' The Lord of Celestials told her, 'The eldest of the hundred sons of Dhrutarashtra, who is known by the name of Duryodhan, will accomplish this business. For his sake, many kings will assemble on the field of Kuru. They will cause one another to be slain in a great war. It is evident, O goddess, that your burden will then be lightened in that battle.' Why then do you, my son, grieve for those *Kshatriyas* that have attained to the highest end? Now arrange for the funeral rites of your sons, grandsons and sires to be performed according to due order!"

Vyas then turned to Gandhari. "I know your heart is rent asunder by the slaughter of your sons, particularly Duryodhan's. But you must not give way to uncontrolled anger. Do not curse your nephews for it was your son's adamant attitude that led to his end."

Then the blind regent with his blindfolded queen and his retinue started for Kurukshetra. Sanjay, Vidur, and Kunti accompanied them. A large number of citizens from the Kuru capital as well as women who had lost their men also travelled with them.

When Yudhisthir received the news that Dhrutarashtra had left for the battlefield with the cortege, he with his brothers prepared to receive him.

"I need to have something collected from Duryodhan's tent before we meet the regent," Krishna said. He whispered instructions to his chariot driver Daruk to pick up an object on the way and join them.

As the Pandavs neared the River Ganga, they heard the laments of the women approaching. When the two parties met on the bank of that great river, emotions ran high. Both parties had lost so many near and dear ones. Yudhisthir, overcome with sympathy rushed forward and bowed. "My lord!"

"I am not king anymore, child," Dhrutarashtra said as he embraced his nephew. Then after an awkward silence of a few moments, he added, "Where are my other nephews? Where is Bheem?"

Bheem stepped forward, but Krishna checked him with a quiet gesture and signalled to Daruk. Daruk quickly produced an object from the chariot and placed it in front of Dhrutarashtra. It was the iron effigy of Bheem, which he had picked up from Duryodhan's tent. As Dhrutarashtra embraced that figure, overcome with anger for the person who had killed all his sons, he tightened his grasp, gnashing his teeth. The metal bent out of shape by the force and Dhrutarashtra cried out as he lost his balance and fell on top of the statue.

"Oh god, what have I done!" His chest and arms bleeding from pressing hard against the twisted metal, Dhrutarashtra said, "I have killed Bheem in my anger!"

"There's no harm done, milord," Krishna said. "It was only an effigy that you crushed. Recollecting yours and your sons' faults, it behoves you to govern your wrath."

Remorseful for what he had done, Dhrutarashtra stood up aided by Sanjay, who had the blood cleaned from Dhrutarashtra' chest and arms.

"When my sons are no more," a mollified Dhrutarashtra muttered, "upon the sons of Pandu depends my happiness."

At a signal from Krishna, Bheem approached and bowed to Dhrutarashtra. This time, the king embraced Bheem, Arjun, Nakul, and Sahdev affectionately. The Pandavs then turned to Gandhari. Her face reflected the turmoil within that she was trying to control.

Sage Vyas approached Gandhari and said, "Do not avail of this opportunity for denouncing a curse. Utilize it for showing forgiveness. Restrain the words that are about to fall from your lips. Remember, whenever your son had besought you saying, 'O mother, bless me,' the answer you always gave him was, 'Thither is victory where righteousness is!' "

"I do not cherish any ill feelings towards the Pandavs, nor do I wish that they should perish," Gandhari replied. "Through the fault of Duryodhan and of Shakuni, and through the action of Karn and Duhshasana, extermination of the Kurus has taken place. But there has been one act done by Bheem in the very presence of Krishna that moves my resentment. He challenged Duryodhan to an encounter with mace, and when he realized that my son was superior to him in skill, he struck the latter below the navel. It is this that moves my wrath."

Bheem in an attempt to soothe her said, "Your son was a superior warrior, milady. I did what I did out of fear for my life, though unrighteous. Duryodhan always used to behave towards us with guile. You know he revealed his left thigh to Draupadi in the hall. You would have never chastised me if I had slain him there and then. Though I held back at the time to honour Yudhisthir's word, I had vowed to punish him by breaking his thigh and that is why I did it."

"You quaffed Dussan's blood!" tears streaked through Gandhari's wet blindfold down her cheek as an artery throbbed at her temples.

"No, milady," Bheem said softly, "I merely touched my lips to his chest and my hands were smeared, for I had vowed so—"

"Why did you not spare even one son of this old couple, one whose offences were lighter? Why did you not leave even one crutch for this blind couple? You caused my only daughter to be a widow." She let out a long breath, and asked, "Where is King Yudhisthir?"

"Your culprit Yudhisthir bows to you," Yudhisthir's voice trembled as he touched her feet. "I deserve your curses, for I am the cause of this destruction. Oh, curse me! I have no longer any need for life, for kingdom, for wealth. Having caused such friends and kin to be slain, I have proved myself to be a great fool."

In an attempt to control her wrath, Gandhari turned her face away. Through a chink that had developed in the blindfold when she wiped her tears, she happened to glimpse Yudhisthir's toenail, which instantly was charred black. The Pandavs were taken aback at the intensity of her deep burning anger. Arjun involuntarily stepped behind Krishna.

"Krishna!" Gandhari turned on Krishna, "Can you hear the piteous cries of my daughters-in-law as they search for their husbands' remains in the mass of dead bodies? Can you hear howls of jackals? Can you hear the flapping of wings of vultures fanning the face of my son that was once fanned by beautiful ladies?" Unable, at last, to contain her anger, Gandhari directed scathing words at Krishna. "You were capable of avoiding this war, yet you let it take place. You are the one responsible for the slaughter of the Kuru clan. It was your advice that led Pandu's children into ignoble acts. I lay my curse on you. You shall witness the destruction of your Yadav clan just as we have witnessed the destruction of ours. You Yadavs too shall fight among yourselves. You shall be the cause of extermination of your kith and kin."

There was a stunned silence after Gandhari had vent her feelings. Krishna did not argue back; he understood the suffering of that poor mother. "So be it!" is all he said.

At last, Dhrutarashtra broke the awkward silence, "Will you arrange for the funeral and last rites of all the slain, Yudhisthir? There are innumerable soldiers whose next of kin are not here."

"Of course, sire," Yudhisthir said, relieved to move away from an uncontrollably sobbing Gandhari.

All the citizens of Hastinapur extended a helping hand. Bodies of those heroes who could be identified were cremated individually. Warriors from both sides without discrimination to the side they had fought for—Duryodhan and Dhrushtadyumna, Dron and Drupad, Shakuni and Virat, Jaidrath and Abhimanyu, Alam and Ghatotkach, Duhshasana and Shikhandi, Laxman and Irawat—they all were cremated on pyres of sandalwood. Bodies mutilated beyond recognition were cremated in mass pyres made from broken chariots. In the stench that pervaded Kurukshetra, flames crackled for days on end devouring the dead with their red-hot tongues.

"Victory looks like defeat to me," a melancholy Yudhisthir said as he watched the mass pyres. "Having won the war, I am obliged to grieve as an afflicted wretch. In reality, I have been doubly defeated. Having caused the death of my kin, I cannot enjoy this sovereignty. I shall retire to the forest and spend my days in meditation. Let Bheem or Arjun be the king."

For days on end, his brothers tried to convince him to enter the capital and assume power. As always, Bheem was forthright in criticizing Yudhisthir for his resigned outlook. "You speak like one who has learned the Vedas by rote, without understanding the meaning! It behoves you not to desert us after you have caused innumerable warriors to be slain. It is your duty now to serve the populace."

Draupadi and Krishna also spoke to him. It was Grandsire Bhishm, whom Yudhisthir visited every evening on his bed of arrows, who convinced him by speaking of his duty to his subjects. Sage Vyas too spoke to Yudhisthir at length and helped dispel Yudhisthir's melancholy thoughts.

A month after the war, realizing he had to shoulder the responsibility, Yudhisthir entered Hastinapur. The spontaneous welcome offered to the Pandavs by the residents of their ancestral capital was heartening. They erected arches, and festooned them with flowering vines and raised banners across the roads in the capital. Soon guests arrived from Dwarika, Virat City, Kampilya and several prominent cities and regions. Arjun's wives, Ulupi from the land of Nagas and Citra from Manipur, arrived at Hastinapur; so did Bheem's wife Hidimba from the realm of giants. A piece of good news came from Abhimanyu's young widow Uttara—she was with child.

"What of the Brahmasra that Ashwatthama has discharged?" Yudhisthir expressed his concern. "Will it destroy the embryo?"

"I will take care of it." Krishna's solemn assurance set his anxiety at rest.

On an auspicious day, in an austere ceremony in the presence of a multitude of sages and citizens, Yudhisthir was crowned king with Krishna pouring holy water on his locks from his conch. Yudhisthir proclaimed Bheem as the crown prince and Arjun the general of their forces.

"You are still the head of Kurus, milord," Yudhisthir's words were like a balm to Dhrutarashtra and Gandhari. "We shall govern the land in your name."

Indeed, Yudhisthir the Just treated his uncle and aunt with great affection and respect; so did Vidur, Krupa, Sanjay, Yuyutsu, and all the Pandavs except Bheem, who was unable to forgive Dhrutarashtra for his past deeds. Bheem often passed comments in the hearing of the blind man denigrating his late sons. Otherwise Dhrutarashtra and Gandhari were cared for and lived in Hastinapur as they always had. Kunti treated Gandhari as her senior. Draupadi, Subhadra, Hidimba, Chitrangada, and Ulupi treated the old couple as if they were their own parents-in-law.

Yudhisthir often visited Kurukshetra to meet Bhishm, who waited for the summer solstice to give up his life. Krishna requested the grandsire to discourse on the duties of the king for the benefit of Yudhisthir. "What more can I tell him, Krishna, when you are there to guide him," Bhishm demurred, but Krishna insisted and the veteran obliged. Bhishm lived for fifty-eight days after the war. His soul left his body happy in the knowledge that Yudhisthir the Just ruled the Elephant City. His passing away on the first day of summer left a great void in Hastinapur. Dhrutarashtra and Yudhisthir performed his last rites on the banks of the holy river.

The months following Yudhisthir's coronation were very challenging for the Pandavs. With the land devastated by war, the economy was in shambles. The coffers of the kingdom were empty.

"Ages ago, a king performed a great sacrifice in the Himalayas," Krishna told Yudhisthir. "He had amassed boundless wealth for distribution to the *Brahmins,* but the *Brahmins,* vowed to simple living, declined those gifts. That treasure lies yet buried there."

The Pandav brothers set out on an expedition to the Himalayan site with Krishna and mined the treasure, which eased the burden on the royal treasury. With that newly acquired wealth, Yudhisthir decided to undertake the great *Ashwamedh* sacrifice to instil new enthusiasm in the populace. A magnificent black stallion was set loose to roam at will and Arjun followed the horse with his troops. He secured the allegiance of every kingdom that the horse visited. On Yudhisthir's orders Arjun installed on the thrones of kingdoms the young sons, wives, or daughters of the kings slain in the Kurukshetra war. Yudhisthir put Dhrutarashtra' name before his on those decrees. Among them was the King Jaidrath's young son, whom Arjun entrusted to Duryodhan's sister Dushala. Working incessantly, Yudhisthir and his brothers rebuilt the empire.

***

After the hectic activity following Yudhishthir's coronation had somewhat subsided, Arjun said to Krishna, as they sat on the palace terrace one night under a canopy of stars, "Krishna, at dawn of the first day on Kurukshetra I had asked you to drive my chariot in the middle of the space dividing the two great armies facing each other. At that moment, as our chariot stood facing east, viewing with awe the majestic figure of the grandsire of the Kurus, clad in white, on his white chariot with the Palmyra standard with five silver stars, a wind began to blow, bearing a shower of pointed pebbles along the ground. I became aware of the tall standards of the combatants, furnished with strings of bells, decked with golden ornaments, garlands of flowers, and rich drapery, and graced with banners were shaken by the wind and emitted loud jingling noises. The Kaurav army trembled at the sight of ferocious Bheem, wielding his mace, stationed in the middle of Pandav troops.

"I blew my Devdutt conch, and you your Panchjanya. The sound of those two conchs filled the welkin. The Kauravs watched our colourful chariot with five white steeds in harness and with the saffron banner of the fierce roaring ape god Hanuman rippling atop. Identifying the divisions from their standards, we surveyed the Kauravs arraigned against us.

"When you, sitting in the chariot driver's seat did not hear any comment from me, you turned to look at me and were surprised to see my ashen face. As you watched, I, with tremulous hands, put the Gandiv bow down.

" 'I can't do this, Krishna,' I said.

" 'Why, Arjun?' you asked.

"And I told you, 'the ones I am facing are my relatives and friends, my teachers and playmates, my dear grandfather and my cousins. I do not wish to slay them even if I am offered the three worlds.' With that I slumped back in the chariot seat.

"You reasoned with me, answered and explained to me. I accepted your words and took up my bow again. However, I confess, I did not fully grasp your reasoning in my agitated state in the midst of the battlefield. Will you explain to me again?

" 'What you need to understand, my friend,' Krishna said ever so gently, 'is that this war was not about you winning a kingdom. It was about fighting for justice. It was about strengthening people's belief in 'justice prevails'. It was about your duty as a *kshatriya* to the citizens of Indraprasth, who want their fair-minded, virtuous king back. It was about your duty to your wife, who lamented over the loss of honour.

"Indeed, you would have failed in your duty if you had decided to pardon the oppressors because they happened to be your relatives. Your cousins cheated a just and worthy king of his kingdom, they assaulted, humiliated and offended the modesty of a chaste woman. They spurned all attempts at peace. One cannot turn a blind eye towards misdeeds just because your friends are among the perpetrators. It does not matter whether one wins the war or loses it, whether one lives or perishes. Performing one's duty conscientiously is what matters.

"There are several paths leading towards salvation of the soul according to each person's bend of mind. One can attain it through deep knowledge of self, or by renouncing the world, or by worship or by action without attachment to the fruit of the action. The last one is suitable for men of action like you.' "

Krishna's words were like a song, soothing and kindling, cajoling and inspiring; and they dispelled Arjun's doubts once and for all. Arjun realized that the need to fight again, was not merely to change one's perspective of the war, but also of life.

***

One morning, Krishna woke to a great commotion in the mansion in the Elephant city. His sister Subhadra rushed into his quarters shouting, "Quick Krishna! That child-slayer Ashwatthama's weapon has struck. Uttara's child is stillborn. Do something: you promised!"

Through the long winding corridors, Krishna flew to Uttara's palace. Kneeling next to the crib, he shut his eyes and placed his palms on the chest of the lifeless infant.

"If I have led a pure life and always strived for the welfare of Arjun, let this child come alive," Krishna said.

A bright light and a rushing sound filled Uttara's room and the newborn baby let out a cry delighting the hearts of Kunti and other women of the royal house.

"Let this grandson of yours be named Parikshit—one who has been tested by time," Krishna told Arjun.

Grand festivities were held in Hastinapur to celebrate

the birth of the sole heir to the Pandavs and the child's great grandfather Indra sent summer showers and a delightful breeze to cool Elephant City. His mission complete, Krishna left for Dwarika soon after Parikshit was born. The Pandavs saw him off with a very heavy heart. Out of great affection, Arjun and Draupadi followed him in their chariot. On the western border of Hastinapur, Krishna signalled his charioteer Daruk to halt and alighted. Arjun and Draupadi walked up to Krishna.

"I am sure we will meet again in the our birth." Krishna smiled. Draupadi did not bother to control her tears. Krishna embraced Arjun and blessed Draupadi before he mounted his chariot again. The couple watched Krishna's chariot rumble away and turn into a tiny silhouette on the western horizon.

18. Dwarika Doomed

"The regent wishes to see you sire," one day Dhrutarashtra's servant approached Yudhisthir with a bow. The king, along with Sage Vyas and Vidur immediately went to see the old regent.

Inviting them to occupy seats in his quarters, Dhrutarashtra said, "When old age arrives it is meet for the members of our race to make over sovereignty to children and lead the forest mode of life."

"You are our foremost of superiors. Without your presence, this palace shall not please me," Yudhisthir said, "Let Yuyutsu, the son of your loins, be made king, or, indeed, anybody else whom you may wish. I shall go into the woods along with you and the queen mother."

"Yudhisthir, let the old king follow the path of all royal sages of old," Vyas advised Yudhisthir, "verily, for all royal sages, retirement into the woods comes at last. Even this is the highest duty of royal sages. They should die either in battle or in the woods agreeably to the scriptures."

Dhrutarashtra said, "In my days I have tried to serve this kingdom. Whether those services have come up to the mark or fallen short of it, it behoves you to forgive me. Duryodhan enjoyed this kingdom without a thorn in his side. Foolish as he was and endued with wicked understanding, he did much wrong to you. Through the fault of my son of wicked understanding, and through his pride, and also through my own faulty policy, a great carnage has taken place of persons of the royal order. Whether I have acted rightly or wrongly, I pray you with joined hands to dispel all remembrance of it from your hearts. This Gandhari also is cheerless and old. Knowing that both of us are afflicted with grief and destitute of children, grant us the permission we seek to retire to the woods."

"You have lived in the palace all your life, milord," Yudhisthir said, "how will you lead the hard life in forest now?"

"For the past year I and Gandhari have been practicing austerities," Dhrutarashtra revealed. "We eat only the simplest of meals once a day and sleep on hard floor."

"I was not aware of this!" an alarmed Yudhisthir exclaimed.

"We did not want you to be unduly worried," Dhrutarashtra smiled, "so we had instructed the servants and maids not to let anyone know."

When Dhrutarashtra and Gandhari declared their intention to retire to the woods, Vidur also decided to join them. Sanjay announced he would accompany to serve them. Dhrutarashtra gave away many presents to the citizens of Hastinapur, who saw the old Kurus off at the gates of the city. Kunti led Gandhari by the hand and Dhrutarashtra walked with his arm around Gandhari's shoulder.

"Where are you going, mother?" Yudhisthir asked when he saw Kunti walking with Gandhari.

"It is time for me to retire too, my son."

"Remember the message you had sent us through Krishna before the war?" Yudhisthir exclaimed, "You said Kshatriya women do not bring forth sons to spend their old age living on charity. You deserve to enjoy the riches with us, mother."

"I only said that so you did not take lying low the insult to Draupadi out of false sense of peace," Kunti's reply was firm. "I have enjoyed all kinds of luxury to the fullest when your father King Pandu ruled the kingdom. Now I want to retire and spend time in peace."

Arrived at Vyas' retreat in deep forest, the four royal old Kurus received initiation into the forest mode of life. Restraining their senses in thought, words and deeds, they began to practise severe austerities and penances like great ascetics. Bearing matted locks on head, and clad in barks, their flesh soon dried up reducing their body to skin and bones. Sanjay waited upon them.

After rains, the Pandavs went to see the elders in the forest along with Draupadi. All the Pandav wives went with them; so did the wives of the deceased princes Duryodhan, Duhshasana and their brothers. They stayed with Dhrutarashtra, Gandhari and Kunti in straw huts in the hermitage.

"Where is Vidur?" Yudhisthir asked of Sanjay.

"He roams the forests and rarely comes to the hermitage."

As they spoke, Yudhisthir saw Vidur's emaciated figure on a hill far away. He quickly ran to meet him. When Vidur saw the king approach, he started running away from him. Yudhisthir gave chase calling out, "Wait, uncle! I am your dear Yudhisthir!"However, Vidur kept moving higher on the hill. At last, Yudhisthir caught up with the old minister. Thoroughly exhausted Vidur stood panting under an old tree. Eyeing the king with a steadfast gaze, he stood motionless in yogic posture. Then using his Yoga-power, Vidur's spirit left his own body and entered the body of Yudhisthir, limb by limb. The just minister united his life-breaths with the just king's life-breaths, and his senses with those of the latter. Yudhisthir saw that life had fled out of Vidur's wizened body. At the same time, he felt that he himself had become stronger than before and that he had acquired many virtues.

Vyas, arriving there, told Yudhisthir that Vidur's body should not be cremated. "Vidur was the eternal Lord of Righteousness incarnate. He has attained the highest regions of felicity. You should not grieve for him at all." Thus addressed, king Yudhisthir returned to the hermitage with Vyas.

"What has happened to my sons after death?" Dhrutarashtra asked Vyas after learning that Vidur had attained a celestial region after passing away.

"They had the honourable end befitting of Kshatriya warriors."

The Pandavs returned to Hastinapur with their retinue. Old Dhrutarashtra and his companions continued to live in the forest. They became wanderers through those woods. Sanjay acted as Dhrutarashtra' guide on uneven land and Kunti became the eye of Gandhari.

One day, they proceeded to a spot deep in the forest. Towards noon, the wind rose high and a fierce forest-conflagration set in. It engulfed that forest all around. Herds of afflicted wild animals escaped to the nearest marshes and waters. Those old royals living on meagre subsistence were incapable of exerting to save themselves. Dhrutarashtra, seeing the conflagration approach him from all sides, addressed Sanjay, "Go, while you can, to a place where the fire may not burn you. As for ourselves, we shall suffer our bodies to be destroyed by this fire and attain to the highest goal."

With great reluctance, Sanjay bid farewell to the three old persons with whom he had spent so much time. As he left for Vyas' abode by the river route, the flames of the forest fire engulfed Dhrutarashtra, Gandhari and Kunti. On his way Sanjay turned several times to look at the evening lit by the forest fire. When he reached Vyas' hermitage, he sent word of the incident to Hastinapur through sage Narad. The Pandavs mourned their beloved mother, aunt and uncle.

On his return to Dwarika, Krishna attended to King Ugrasen and the long neglected confederation of Yadav tribes of Andhak, Vrishni and Bhoj. While the Pandavs prospered in Hastinapur under Yudhisthir, under Krishna's guidance the Yadavs achieved great prosperity in Dwarika. They thrived on the west coast, while the Pandavs prospered in the north. For its riches, Dwarika came to be known as the 'City of Gold' and the 'Amravati on earth'.

Thirty-six years passed and gradually the prosperity of Yadavs turned into decadence. Abnegating responsibility, young Yadav men and women indulged in voluptuary pursuits. They loved their drink and dance more than was good for them and led licentious lives.

It was in this hedonistic atmosphere that a team of savants under Sage Narad and Durvas happened to visit Dwarika. The vivant youngsters of the city saw the visitors and decided to have some fun. Krishna's young son Samba was among the merrymakers. That dreamboat of a boy donned a long-flowing, luxurious silk garment padding his belly under the raiment and surrounded by his friends presented himself as an enceinte lady to those sages.

"This wife of Babhru is expecting, sires," the boy's friends told the sages, "Can you predict what offspring she will bear–son or daughter?"

The sages were not taken in by Samba's disguise; they execrated the flippant ways of the young Yadavs. "This heir of Krishna will bear a fierce iron bolt, which will be the exterminator of your race," the unexpected curse from the ever-irritable sage Durvas stunned the youngsters.

When Dwarika's King Ugrasen learned what had transpired, he conferred with Balram and Krishna. Remembering Gandhari's curse, Krishna merely said, "What is destined will happen."

Next morning Samba brought forth an iron bolt, terrible to behold. The news spread like wildfire through Dwarika. King Ugrasen ordered the iron bolt pulverised and the powder dispersed in the sea. The powder floated to the coast and rushes sprouted where it landed on the beach. To ward off further evil, the King by a decree, prohibited production and consumption of intoxicants in the walled city.

While the Yadavs were thus endeavouring to avoid the impending calamity, the embodied form of Father Time every day wandered about their houses. He appeared in the form of a man of terrible and fierce aspect. Of a bald head and bushy eyebrows, he was of tawny complexion. Sometimes people saw him as he peered into their houses. Mighty bowmen among the Yadavs shot shafts at him, but none of them succeeded in piercing him, for he was none else than the Destroyer of all creatures. Day by day strong winds blew, and many were the awful and evil omens that arose, foreboding the destruction of the Yadavs.

The streets swarmed with rats and mice. At night, they ate away the hair and nails of slumbering men. Sparrows chirped, sitting within houses. The noise made by those birds ceased not for even a short while by day or by night. The cranes imitated the hooting of the owl, and goats imitated the cries of jackals. In the eateries, upon food that was clean and well boiled, when served out for eating, were found innumerable worms. Earthen pots showed cracks or broke from no apparent cause.

The young insulted the aged. Men and women committed sinful acts. They lusted and fornicated without any shame. At that time, the women in Dwarika dreamed every night that a demoness of blue complexion and white teeth with hair loose, entering their abodes, laughed aloud and ran through the city, snatching from them the auspicious threads in their wrists. The men dreamt that terrible vultures, entering their houses and fire-chambers, gorged themselves on their bodies.

Thinking upon the omens that the Death Lord showed, Krishna understood that the destined year had come, and that what Gandhari had said, burning with grief on account of the death of her sons, and deprived of all her kinsmen, was about to transpire. On his advice, the Yadavs undertook a journey to the seacoast for bathing in the sacred waters of the ocean. The Yadavs prepared diverse kinds of viands and meat and wines, despite the prohibition. Along with their families, the troops of the Yadavs in their ceremonial garbs then set out with enthusiasm from the city on cars and steeds and elephants. King Ugrasen remained in the city with some old people. Reaching the spot called Prabhas on the west coast the Yadavs took up residence in the vacation habitation on the beach stocked with provisions.

As soon as Krishna dismounted from his car at Prabhas and his driver Daruk got down to unhitch the car, the four famous horses all of a sudden bolted with the empty car drawing it into the Western sea and disappeared forever. Balram left the company, went to a secluded spot further up the coast, and rested there in yoga.

That night the Yadavs lit bonfires along the coast and started a party. Booze flowed freely. Women lay cuddled with their men on the beach. Some damsels swayed and swung to blaring instruments. Light banter suddenly took a serious turn and heated debate about the war started between Krutavarma and Satyaki, who had fought on opposite sides at KuruXetra.

"What Kshatriya worth his salt would participate in the cowardly massacre of the sleeping Pandavs?" Satyaki taunted Krutavarma.

"...And you participated in the immoral killing of Dron and Karn!" Krutavarma retorted.

Krishna's wife Satyabhama had a grudge against Krutavarma for he had once wronged her father. As she sat in Krishna's lap, Satyabhama reminded him of the incident and Krishna rebuked Krutavarma. Satyaki challenged Krutavarma and they came to blows. In an inebriated state Satyaki drew a cutlass and slew Krutavarma. The Bhojas and Andhaks were infuriated at that; together they attacked Satyaki of the Vrishni clan with cooking pans. Seeing Satyaki reel under that attack, Pradyumn, Krishna's son from Rukmini rushed to aid him and the assailants turned on him too. Before Krishna could intervene, both Satyaki and Pradyumn lay dead with their heads bashed in by those thick metal pots. In a rage, Krishna uprooted the rushes growing on the coast and hurled them at his son's slayers. No sooner did those stems leave his hand, they turned into the iron bolts from which they had sprung, killing a score of the Bhojas and Andhaks. Then it was a drunken free for all. The Yadavs uprooted the rushes, which turned into iron bolts and slew each other with them. In less than an hour, all the Yadav men lay dead on the coast. Only Krishna, his driver Daruk, the women and children survived.

"Go to Hastinapur and inform the Kurus that Gandhari's curse has come true. The Yadavs are destroyed," Krishna told Daruk. "Ask Arjun to come to Dwarika immediately and take our womenfolk to the Elephant City with him."

Krishna escorted the Yadav families to Dwarika, and met the old king.

"Just as I witnessed the slaughter of the Kurus, I have today witnessed the slaughter of the Yadavs by in-fighting. This metropolis, which I once helped build and prosper, has the appearance of a necropolis now. Devoid of all those heroes, who were like brothers unto me, I cannot bear to live here. Please take care of the women and children until Arjun arrives from Hastinapur. I will now leave for the coast where Balram is resting in the forest in yog. I shall practice penances in his company."

Having bowed to the king, Krishna left Dwarika with a heavy heart. By dawn, he reached the woods on the coast where Balram sat in meditation. As Krishna approached him, he saw a great white snake issue out of Balram's mouth. It proceeded to the ocean where Vasuki, Takshak and several foremost of serpents along with Varun, the lord of the sea, received it. On the coast Balram's body turned lifeless as his spirit left in the form of Shesha the five-headed snake that dwelt in the milk of ocean serving its Lord Vishnu. It had protected Krishna and saw him through a childhood full of hazards.

After witnessing that sight, Krishna wandered through the forest. He had thought of this situation when Gandhari had cursed him. Having seen the end of the Kurus and now that of his own relatives, he reckoned his time had arrived too. He lay down with his feet crossed, in deep yogic meditation on the bare ground in a thicket on the coast. Presently, a hunter arrived in that part of the wood. With Krishna's supine form half-hidden by bushes, the hunter mistook the soles of Krishna's crossed feet for a deer's ears and shot an arrow, which entering Krishna's in-step, ploughed all the way. The hunter, when he arrived to collect his prey, was stunned to see a handsome dark person clad in cream robes hit by his arrow. Trembling at the thought that he was guilty of manslaughter, he bowed to Krishna. Comforting the guilt-ridden man, Krishna rose upwards filling the entire welkin with splendour. Celestial sages and the leaders of the celestial beings – deities, Gandharvs, Apsaras, Yakshs and Kinnars accompanied Indra in receiving Krishna at Svarg's entrance. They bowed to him while the celestial musicians hymned his praises. Spending some time in their company, shortly he ascended to his own inconceivable region in the highest echelons of Svarg.

King Ugrasen, on receiving the news of Krishna's departure from earth from the hunter's arrow, spent anxious days waiting for Arjun in Dwarika. Apprehensive that the enemies of Yadavs would seize the opportunity to attack Dwarika, guarded by only the very young and very old, he ordered the city gates shut. Even nature seemed to have turned an adversary. Fierce wind blew, dark clouds rumbled from the sea and the waters around the island city turned turbulent.

At Hastinapur when the Pandavs received the disastrous news from Daruk, they immediately dispatched Arjun to fetch the Yadav survivors. The womenfolk set up a loud wail, when Arjun reached Dwarika. Apart from the Yadav women, there resided in that island city the sixteen thousand women whom Satyabhama and Krishna had rescued from the demon king Narakasur. Although he was himself afflicted with grief, Arjun somehow consoled those women. He also met Krishna and Balram's father Vasudev. The old man had given up food and had turned into a mere skeleton. Arjun then called on King Ugrasen.

"On the seventh day I shall leave for Hastinapur along with all women and families, milord," Arjun told his plan, "please have ready as many chariots as possible to transport the people."

"Yes, it was Krishna's wish that you should escort the families. However, I will not leave this dear city come whatever may," Ugrasen declared.

Arjun went to the coast and witnessed the sight of bodies scattered all around and arranged for the funeral. He sought out Krishna and Balram's bodies and brought them back to Dwarika. Back in the island city, he found Krishna's father Vasudev had passed away too. They were cremated on pyres of sandalwood.

As planned, on the seventh day a great convoy left Dwarika in carriages drawn by whatever draught animal could be mustered; horses, mules, donkeys, camels and oxen were pressed into service. The old King stood on the turret watching them leave by the gate towards the mainland. As each car left the city, Ugrasen saw on the seaward side the waves rise higher and higher and drown the trees on the coast where ducks and cranes lived. When the last of the cars passed out of the massive gates, the waves rose above the city walls of adamant, flooded the boat gardens and rushed into the streets. Already at some distance in the lead car of the caravan, Arjun heard a great rumble and as he turned to look, the entire island of Dwarika with its domes and towers, sank underwater.

Leaders of the Mleccha clans in the Abhira kingdoms of the land of five rivers held an emergency meeting in the night. They had word that a large convoy carrying the Yadav women along with the treasury was moving from Dwarika towards Hastinapur.

"They have little protection..." their informer was breathless with excitement, "...only half a dozen men accompany all those voluptuous beauties of the Yadavs!"

The meeting unanimously decided on a raid. Hordes of Mleccha riders converged overnight on a chosen stretch of road passing through a hilly pass in dense forest. Lining the several miles long path on both sides, they rested in ambush while their scouts on treetops at regular intervals waited for the convoy to arrive.

Towards mid-morning the next day, scouts sighted the advance cars of the slow-moving convoy and alerted their main force. The Mlecchas had rested while waiting and were ready for action. They let the lead car with the Hastinapur flag and armed men go past the far end of the ravine. When the main body of the caravan was in the middle of the ambush, at a signal from the leader, they charged to the sound of blaring horns, cutting off the lead and rear cars that contained armed people. The attack came as a complete surprise and the caravan halted abruptly as the animals reared in harness.

Arjun, at the head of the caravan, quickly picked up his Gandiv bow, but he could not bend it, it felt extraordinarily rigid. When, at last, he managed to bend it, the string snapped. He succeeded in stringing the bow on his third attempt. As he touched his inexhaustible quivers, he was flabbergasted to find no arrows in them. He pronounced the chants for his celestial weapons but none appeared. Utterly confused by this strange development, he picked up a spear and jumped from his chariot. Krishna's grandson Vajra joined him. They took up position facing the Mleccha warriors at the mouth of the chasm. With great difficulty, the two managed to prevent the raiders from reaching the first three cars, which bore Krishna's wives Satyabhama and Rukmini among other royal women of the Yadavs. The guards at the rear of the caravan also protected the last couple of cars.

The Mlecchas had a field day with the unprotected main body of the caravan. Riding up and down by the side of the cars, their leaders took their pick of the svelte and the sultry. Some women presenting spirited struggles succumbed in the end; some meek by nature, submitted silently; while the amatory among the Yadav women willingly embraced their brawny, swarthy captors. The raiders, after they had their fill, unhitched the horses from the Yadav carriages and loaded the caskets of treasure on their backs. Of those premier women captured, the bellicose ones travelled in bonds whereas the acquiescent ones rode with their new lords on their mounts.

When the marauders galloped away with their precious acquisitions in his very sight, Arjun assembled the remainder of his charge. Though he was quite dispirited himself due to his failed weapons, he managed to console and cajole them to continue the journey towards Hastinapur. All along the route, Arjun brooded on the calamity that had struck him and the Yadavs. For the first time he felt as old as the eighty years of his age – senescent and dotard. Though cheerless, with dogged determination the caravan trudged on after discarding those cars whose horses or occupants were taken by the raiders.

After travelling a week, they reached KuruXetra. Arjun established the sons of Yadavs in different parts of the Kuru kingdom – Krutavarma's son at Martika with the remaining Bhoj women, the son of Satyaki along with the women and children of his clan on the banks of Saraswati, and he placed Krishna's grandson Vajra at the helm of Indraprasth. Krishna's wives Satyabhama and Rukmini retired to the woods.

Having fulfilled his duty to the Yadavs, a desolate Arjun went to see Sage Vyas in his hermitage on the Ganga. Seeing the son of Kunti in great despair, the sanguine sage made him sit comfortably. Vyas lent a sympathetic ear to Arjun's monologue of woe.

"The Yadavs have slaughtered each other in a drunken brawl. They have been slain with the blades of grass. Krishna and Balram have ascended to Svarg. The golden city of Dwarika lies at the bottom of the ocean... and I failed to protect the Yadav women. The Mlecchas of Abhiras kingdom in the land of five rivers took thousands of Yadav women right in front of my eyes! And I stood helpless, unable even to string my bow. My weapons have failed me!I fail to derive peace of mind. I desire not to live in this world. Reft of Krishna's company what have I to live for? O, omniscient one, please tell me what is good for me now, for I am now a wanderer with an empty heart, despoiled of my kinsmen and of my possession."

"The mighty Yadav warriors have been destroyed by the curse of Gandhari and Durvas. That which has happened had been ordained," Vyas spoke in a calming voice. "All this has Time for its root. Time is, indeed, the seed of the universe, Arjun. It is Time again, that withdraws everything at its pleasure. One becomes mighty, and, again, losing that might, becomes weak. One becomes a master and rules others, and, again, losing that position, becomes a servant for obeying the behests of others. Your weapons, having achieved success, have gone away to the place they came from. The time has come for you Pandavs to attain to the highest goal. Even this is what I regard to be highly beneficial for you all."

A thoughtful Arjun, with Vyas' permission, returned to the capital city named after the elephant. He went straight to King Yudhisthir and narrated back to his brothers all that had happened in Dwarika and on the way.

"It is Time that cooks every creature in his cauldron," Yudhisthir said contemplating on all that had transpired, "I think that what has happened is due to the cords of Time with which he binds us all."

"Indeed, it's Time..." Arjun started.

"...for us to retire too," Yudhisthir completed what Arjun had started saying.

With his brothers' and Draupadi's concurrence he announced his intention of retiring to the woods as Dhrutarashtra had done before him. The citizen of Hastinapur were saddened that this just king who had ruled them so well for almost four decades, was going to retire and tried to dissuade him from the thought. However, Yudhisthir, now an octogenarian, was firm on his resolve. Ulupi, Citra and Hidimba also resolved to leave for the realms of their respective clans.

Yudhisthir had all arrangements made for retirement. He assigned roles to Krupa, Dhrutarashtra' sole surviving son Yuyutsu, Arjun's wife Subhadra, Abhimanyu's wife Uttara and her son Parikshit.

"Let Krupa be the preceptor to Parikshit. Let Parikshit rule Hastinapur after me. I entrust the king and kingdom to your care, Yuyutsu. Let Uttara under Subhadra's guidance, as the queen-mother take care of the King."

The sight of the five brothers leaving Hastinapur with Draupadi attired in simple clothes made from tree bark evoked old citizens' memories of the day when they had left for the forest after their defeat in the gambling match at the hands of Shakuni. A stray dog followed the Pandavs as they left the capital. The seven of them travelled east, and reached the coast. At the sea with red water, a demon with fiery red hair blocked their way.

"No weapons are allowed here," he announced, pointing to the Gandiv and the twin inexhaustible quivers that Arjun carried. Out of attachment, Arjun had retained the celestial weapon although it served him no more. On hearing the words of the yaksh, he unslung and handed over the legendary bow and quivers.

"I am indeed the Fire God," the being said receiving the

great bow, "I had given these weapons to you and the disc to Krishna at the time of burning the Khandav forest. The disc has already disappeared from earth. The role of these weapons is over for this era. It is time for returning them to Varun."

They travelled south along the coastline to the end of the peninsula, and then turned northwest. On the west coast, off Prabhas, they gazed wistfully at the submerged city of Dwarika several feet under water. When the sea was calm and the weather clear, they tried to discern landmark buildings they had seen before.

"Unto Time I bow!" Yudhisthir said.

With a heavy heart, they turned north towards the Himalayas. Having crossed several hermitages and met renowned sages, they reached Badri where half a century ago they had rendezvoused with Arjun after his sojourn in heaven.

"That's where I found the golden Saugandhika flower!" a reminiscent Draupadi pointed the spot to Bheem.

"If one has led a truly righteous life," Yudhisthir said, engrossed in contemplation, "then one can attain the Elysium in the human body. Let us take the path to Svarg."

They bid farewell to the sages and crossed the Scented Hills. As they proceeded on their northward journey, days turned cold and nights were freezing. With dogged determination, the seven travellers crossed the snow-clad hills and entered a vast icy desert. Draupadi, lean from exertion, was the first one to fall.

"Such a chaste woman, why did she fall?" Bheem asked of Yudhisthir.

"Indeed, she never indulged in a sinful act," Yudhisthir replied. "However, although we were all equal to her, in her heart she loved Arjun more than us. That one act of hers has caused her fall."

Bheem went to where Draupadi had fallen.

"Let me give you a hand," he said. "I will carry you on my back."

He had to bend on all fours and bring his ear next to her lips to hear her feeble words in the howling wind.

"No, please. My time has come. You have done all you could for me. I am so grateful," she said gasping for breath in the rare air at that altitude. "But there is one thing I want you to do for me – take birth as the eldest brother in your next birth and not as the middle one!"With great difficulty, Bheem left her side when she shut her eyes one last time and her bosom stopped heaving.

The next to fall that cold afternoon was Sahdev. "He was so dedicated to you. Why did he fall?" Bheem asked.

"He was an excellent astronomer," Yudhisthir said, "but he thought there was no one superior to him in intellect. His pride caused the fall."

They had gone only a few paces, when Nakul collapsed.

"Why did he fall?"

"He was so very handsome, but he thought there was no one more handsome than him in the three worlds. His vanity was the cause of his fall."

The remaining three brothers and their dog trudged on in silence. It was Arjun's turn next.

"He too?"

"For he thought there was none as good with weapons as he and had proclaimed that he will defeat all the Kaurav warriors, but failed to keep his promise. That was his undoing."

The desert turned darker at the approach of the night. In the ensuing twilight, Bheem fell with a thud that shook the ice all around.

"I always obeyed you, even when I disagreed... then why..." Bheem looked at Yudhisthir with the question in his eyes.

"You were the most powerful of all combatants," Yudhisthir sighed, "but when you sat for your meal, you never bothered to know if the others had eaten or not. It's your gluttony that caused your fall, wolf-belly."

Only the hound walked at Yudhisthir's heels giving him company in the lonely expanse of deathly white in the growing dark. Then a light appeared over the horizon at the north and Indra in his glowing chariot with its winged horses gracefully swooped down and alighted in front of Yudhisthir.

"Come, O Just King!" Indra invited Yudhisthir to the chariot. "Come with me to Svarg, you deserve a place there!"

Yudhisthir placed a weary foot on the chariot step and the dog followed, wagging its tail happily.

"Not the dog!" Indra tried to shoo the mutt away. "Dogs

are not allowed in Svarg..."

"If the dog can't go, neither will I!" Yudhisthir took retracted his foot from the chariot step, "It has kept me company all through the journey; I won't leave it here in this dead cold desert."

"You will give up eternal life in Svarg for a mongrel?" Indra was aghast.

"Have no doubt about that," was Yudhisthir's calm reply.

There was a flash and Dharm the Lord of Justice appeared where the dog had been a moment ago.

"I am so pleased with you, my son," Dharm said as Yudhisthir bowed to his father. "I wanted to test your compassion, Yudhisthir."

They both mounted Indra's celestial chariot. With its flying coloured banners and the pennons streaming from the flagpoles, Indra's car swooped through the gates of Svarg, past the white elephant Airavat. Sage Narad, with the Gandharv band playing melodious music in the background, welcomed Yudhisthir. As he entered the great hall of Indra's court, his eyes fell upon a warrior seated on a majestic chair and served by Apsaras.

"Duryodhan! What is he doing in Svarg?"Yudhisthir was flabbergasted.

"He died the honourable death of a true Kshatriya, didn't he?" Narad quipped.

"He was stained by cupidity and possessed of little foresight. It was for him that friends, and kinsmen, over the whole Earth were slaughtered by us whom he had afflicted greatly in the deep forest. It was for him that the virtuous princess of Panchal, Draupadi of faultless features, our wife, was dragged into the midst of the assembly before all our seniors," Yudhisthir was indignant. "Ye gods, I have no desire to even behold him. I wish to go to the place where my brothers and wife live."

"It does not behove you to be angry in Svarg. You should not recall the deeds on earth here. This is heaven. All enmities cease here," Narad said mildly.

"If this Wight has attained these regions, I wish to see what regions my valiant brothers and friends have attained. I do not see Bheem, Arjun, Satyaki, Dhrushtadyumna and

Shikhandi here."

"Why, you can surely go to the parts assigned to your family and friends, I think."Narad looked at Indra, who motioned to a guard who bowed to Yudhisthir and said, "This way, my lord."

They left by a side door onto a path that wound through dense trees. It soon turned dark and the path became uneven. A repulsive stench arose as they went further. Like moss, human hair covered the path, slippery with flesh and blood. Rotting corpses, with entrails hanging out, lined the way on both sides. Gadflies hovered and worms wiggled all over. Evil spirits resided in corpses hanging upside down from trees with knotted branches and leaves with pointed ends as sharp needles. They came across a river of boiling oil, difficult to cross. On its banks, sinful men were being tortured on racks of iron.

Beholding that foul region, Yudhisthir asked the celestial guide, "How far do we go by this path? What is this region? Where are my brothers?"

"The path ends here. I have been directed to bring you here," the being replied, "But if you wish to go back to Indra's court, you may come with me."

Confused, Yudhisthir decided to return and as he turned around, he heard cries from the dark surroundings.

"Milord, do stay a little bit longer with us. Your presence has dispelled the foul stench and brought a breath of fresh air. Great has been the relief to us by your arrival, torments have ceased to afflict us."

Yudhisthir stood still. Those voices were familiar, but he could not place them immediately as they seemed distorted with pain.

"Who are you? Why do you stay here?" he asked.

"I am Bheem!" "I am Arjun!" "I am Karn!" "I am Nakul and here is Sahdev!" "I am your queen Draupadi!" "I am Dhrushtadyumna!"

"What perverse destiny is this?" The answers stunned Yudhisthir. "What are those sinful acts which were committed by those high-souled beings, Karn and the sons of Draupadi, and the princes of Panchal, so that their residence has been assigned in this region of foetid smell and great woe? And what is that act by which Duryodhan has attained that delightful dwelling? I cannot believe what I witness. Am I asleep or awake? Am I conscious or unconscious? Or, is all this mental delusion due to disorders of the brain?" Then turning to the celestial messenger, in indignation he said, "Return to the presence of those whose messenger you are. Tell them that I shall not go back to the luxuries of Svarg, but shall stay here, since, these afflicted brothers of mine have become comforted by my presence."

The celestial messenger returned to Indra's court with this message from Yudhisthir. The Chief of Celestials along with the Lord of Justice and other deities immediately came over to the spot where Yudhisthir had remained with his brothers. At their arrival, the darkness that had enveloped that region disappeared and the terrible sights of mangled corpses and tortured sinners vanished. A delightfully perfumed, cool breeze started flowing.

"You have attained success, my son," Yamadharm said to Yudhisthir, "Your very last test is over; the illusions have ended. The eternal regions of felicity are yours. Every king has to see Hell. He who enjoys the fruits of his good acts must afterwards visit Hell; he who sees Hell first shall afterwards enjoy Heaven. He whose sinful acts are many enjoys Heaven first and Hell later. He whose sins are few and pious deeds many, sees Hell first and then Heaven. After spending time in Heaven and Hell proportionate to their good and bad deeds, souls go back to earth for their next birth.

"It is for this, I had you sent for having a view of Hell first. You had deceived Dron in the matter of his son. That is why you have seen Hell by an act of deception. Similarly, Bheem, Arjun and Draupadi, have seen the place of sinners. Come now, all of you have been cleansed of your sins. All those kings who had aided you and who laid their life in battle have all attained to Heaven. Meet also those of your ancestors of yore, who have attained the cherished regions. Come and behold them!"

Then Yudhisthir with his brothers and wife was led by the Lord of Celestials to delightful parts of Amravati city. There they took their rightful place among the foremost of noble and meritorious souls from various epochs and led an exalted life in the company of their dear ones.

***

About the Author

Sudhir Joglekar, is an author of novels and short stories, a translator, and a freelance columnist. He regularly writes articles in renowned magazines and periodicals. He writes in English, Hindi and Marathi. His topics of interest are movies, literature and cultural issues.

He is acommercial printer by profession and has received awards at the state level. He lives in the city of Belagavi in the state of Karnataka in India.

His blog on The Mahabharat can be accessed on http://riddlesinmahabharat.blogspot.com/

BOOKS IN THE SERIES

*

ADVENTURES OF THE PANDAV PRINCES

(Focuses on the story of the Pandav brothers culminating in the Kurukshetra war)

*

THE KRISHNA CHRONICLES

(Focuses on the story of Krishna from birth to the rise and fall of Dwarika)

*

Forthcoming

KINGS OF YORE

(Stories of the ancestors of the Kuru and Yadu clans.)

When King Pandu meets his end from the terrible Curse of the Deer in the Snow Mountains his queen and sons decide to return to their capital. Little do the Pandav Princes know that before they can claim their legacy they have to face evil lurking in dark corridors of the palace, escape infernos and live in wilderness, combat cannibals, marry giantesses and win princesses, descend to the Netherworld and ascend to the Elysium.

After their queen is publicly humiliated in the blind King's court and justice denied they face an apocalyptic, fratricidal war which threatens to devastate the realm on the cusp of ages, and questions their very belief in ethics. But the Pandavs are no ordinary humans. Born with the blessings of Celestial lords, they have the charismatic Krishna as their friend, philosopher, and guide who can steer them through the calamities that befall them. Or, can he?

Retold for young readers, the stories from one of the world's oldest and longest epic Mahabharat abound in a wealth of multi-faceted characters and variegated worldviews.

www.ingramcontent.com/pod-product-compliance
Lightning Source LLC
Chambersburg PA
CBHW050016170726
48282CB00025B/428
9788196713119